BLISS
MONTAGE

BLISS
MONTAGE
LING MA

Farrar, Straus and Giroux

New York

Farrar, Straus and Giroux
120 Broadway, New York 10271

Several of these stories originally appeared, in slightly different
form, in the following publications: *Granta* ("Los Angeles"), *Zoetrope* ("G"),
Unstuck ("Yeti Lovemaking"), *The Atlantic* ("Office Hours"), *The New Yorker*
("Peking Duck"), and *The Virginia Quarterly Review* ("Tomorrow").

Library of Congress Cataloging-in-Publication Data
Names: Ma, Ling, 1983– author.
Title: Bliss montage / Ling Ma.
Description: First edition. | New York : Farrar, Straus and Giroux, 2022.
Identifiers: LCCN 2022021733 | ISBN 9780374293512 (hardcover)
Subjects: LCGFT: Novels.
Classification: LCC PS3613.A14 B55 2022 | DDC 813/.6—dc23
LC record available at https://lccn.loc.gov/2022021733

Designed by Gretchen Achilles

www.fsgbooks.com
www.twitter.com/fsgbooks • www.facebook.com/fsgbooks

1   3   5   7   9   10   8   6   4   2

to Daniela

Contents

BLISS
MONTAGE

Los Angeles

The house in which we live has three wings. The west wing is where the Husband and I live. The east wing is where the children and their attending au pairs live. And lastly, the largest but ugliest wing, extending behind the house like a gnarled, broken arm, is where my 100 ex-boyfriends live. We live in LA.

Our house has the nicest view in the Hills. From our Spanish-tiled kitchen, I can see my old apartment complex down the hill, a coral stucco converted motel. The burned-out sign says EL PARAISO. Another girl lives in my studio now. In T-shirt and slip, she drinks a glass of juice, stands hunched over the sink in the kitchen that I painted seafoam green. It is three in the morning, it is three in the afternoon.

She is there, I am here, and all my ex-boyfriends who dated me there are also here. Aaron. Adam. Akihiko. Alejandro. Anders. Andrew. Those are just the *A*s.

My 100 ex-boyfriends and I hang out every day. We get into the Porsche 911 Turbo S, bunching into it as if it were a clown car, and drive down roads and boulevards, hills and canyons, palm-frond-strewn avenues, and parking garages of shopping malls. Geoff drives. The city sprawls out endlessly. Bougainvillea the color of bruises grows across people's fences. Sometimes, a bamboo grove. Sometimes, a cemetery. Sometimes, a free clinic devoted to the removal of burst capillaries. The sun hits our faces, our eyes squint in the light, our hair billows in the wind.

On the Husband's credit card: 101 burgers at Umami Burger, 101 admission tickets to LACMA, 101 golden milks at Moon Juice. We go shopping. We go to Barneys. We go to Koreatown. We go to Urth Caffé to do some light reading.

Can I get an extra wheatgrass shot? Benoît says.

Does this hoodie make me look fat? Fred says.

It's almost time for us to go home, Chang says.

And Aaron, he doesn't say anything. Neither does Adam.

It is almost evening by the time we return to our gated community, the sky a layer cake of pinks and oranges. At the security booth, a black iron gate lifts for us, heavy with its own weight.

After we've disembarked, the Husband returns home from the investment firm. He comes in quietly, through our noiseless garage door. I know it's him when I hear the sound of ice clinking against glass, then bourbon pouring, glugging as it leaves the bottle. He lets it sit for a bit.

Hi, honey, I say. How was your day?

$$$$, $$$$$$$$$, he says. $$$$$$$$$$$$$$.

Well, did it go up or down?

$$$$$$$$$$.

Does that mean you're working this weekend?

$.

The Husband is a resting place. He is a chair. Sometimes I drape myself over him and I get the physical comfort of not being alone. I can feel it anytime I want; mostly Saturday nights, mostly Sunday mornings. But the times I need it most are the early evenings when I feel like I am dissolving. During this time, my ex-boyfriends scatter, and the Husband and I go somewhere for dinner.

I put on my plane coat, and we take the time-share jet up to Marin County. By eight, we descend into Sausalito, where Danielle Steel lives, where moody conifers grow on steep hills, and the expanse of the deep bay laps at rocks along the shore. It's pretty here, but the only place to shop is Benetton.

At the slow-food restaurant on the harbor, an older couple at the next table beams our way. It takes a moment to see that we look like a younger version of them, sans their matching sweater vests and silvered hair. Between our tables, a span of thirty years. I return their smiles and look away.

The Husband orders a red wine and I order a Diet Coke. Plates are laid out: tuna carpaccio encrusted with toasted sesame seeds, pea shoot tendrils tenderly clasping veal medallions in abstracted herb sauce, zucchini slivers dressed with mint-dill reduction.

The Husband sips his wine, eats his veal while I tell him about the things my ex-boyfriends and I did all day, the art we saw, the items we bought. Dessert arrives, a vanilla torte with raspberry coulis and mascarpone cream.

I try to enjoy it, but I can't seem to escape the gaze of the couple at the next table. The wife, she can't help herself. She leans over, puts her hand on my wrist, says, You will produce beautiful children.

That's been done, I tell her, taking my hand away.

I have one son and one daughter, one gang-bangingly after the other. One is six and the other seven. They look and act so much like the Husband. They chew with their mouths closed, they know the correct fork to use. At night, they crawl into my lap, full of easily disclosed secrets, light as folding chairs.

At home, when the daughter spills raspberry juice on the carpet, the son chides, This is why we can't have nice things.

No, that's not true, I tell them, looking at the daughter. You can have everything.

Really? she asks.

There is nothing you ever have to give up, I say, pretty sure this is the wrong thing to say to a six-year-old but saying it anyway. You can have your cake and eat it too.

I can have my juice and spill it too?

Sure. Good use of analogy.

My ex-boyfriends take turns teaching the kids new things. They practice piano, solve math exercises, demonstrate logic and rhetoric.

Find middle C, Philippe says.

Solve for x, Akihiko says.

If a, then b, Hans says.

But Aaron, he doesn't say anything. Neither does Adam.

There are 100 ex-boyfriends, but two that really matter. Their names are similar: Aaron and Adam. Adam and Aaron. Aaron because I was in love, Adam because he beat me. I met Adam first, then Aaron. The wound, then the salve. Maybe you don't know that you're wounded until you receive the salve. The salve that makes everything come back. After you get beaten, you don't go out. Your face swells into a snout. You don't buy Tylenol or groceries, because you'd look like an animal loosened onto the streets. Animal control would mistake you for something else. Instead, I stayed indoors. I washed the blood off the walls and the sheets. The splattered pillow I kept as evidence, not for anyone else, just for myself. I listened to music. Cat Power, *The Covers Record*. I caught up on my reading. From *Primer to Abuse*: Practiced abusers don't hit a woman in the face. The novice abuser is pushed to it only by extreme, uncontrollable conditions. I read it again. Not "conditions"; "emotions." I brushed up on philosophy: To live is to exist within time. To remember is to negate time.

All of my remembering begins late in the afternoon and lasts late into the night. How do I know, Adam once asked be-

7

fore he struck me, if what you feel is real? And not something you felt for everyone else that came before? And everyone that will come after?

After dinner, the Husband and I take the time-share back to LA. It is dark as we sweep across the wingspan of California. Below us, the lights go on, city by city, time passing. LA is so beautiful at night from afar, a constellation of stars. It sprawls out and around, not so much a city as a series of urban planning decisions made without foresight. Frank Lloyd Wright mansions give way to Le Corbusier–style churches, mid-century bungalows cohabit with Mediterranean villas, pleasure palaces rub up against ascetic lifestyle centers. There is no pattern, there is no meaning.

Beneath the plane blanket, the Husband's hand finds mine.

$$$$$$$$$$$$$$$$? he asks.

How can I not be? I answer, and squeeze his hand.

When we return to the house, the kids are both asleep. The Husband retreats to our bedroom, and I to the guest cottage, where I spend most nights. We used to rent it, but it's empty now. A winding stone path leads me there through the sprawling backyard, through thickets of bougainvillea bushes sneezing with pollinic blooms. The cottage is furnished with pieces that previous tenants left behind: a chair, a bed, a treadmill. I open up the windows and walk on the treadmill while reading old issues of fashion magazines.

Someone knocks on the door.

Come in, I say.

The door swings opens. It's Aaron.

I thought you weren't talking to me, I say.

I need a ride. Will you drive me?

Get Geoff. He's probably awake.

No, just you, please. What are you doing?

Exercising.

He clears his throat. I'm leaving.

Leaving where?

Leaving here. I'm moving out.

My breath catches.

You can't say that you didn't expect this, Aaron says. Everyone's overstayed.

They're welcome to overstay.

C'mon. He gestures for me to follow, and I follow. The Porsche idles in the driveway. He opens the driver's door for me and I get in. The keys are already in the ignition. The dashboard clock indicates it's just after midnight.

Where are your bags? I ask.

In the trunk.

There's not much more I can say. Wordlessly, we drive downhill, past other people's estates. At the base of the hill, I swipe my ID card and the black iron gates open triumphantly, a bird preparing for flight.

Where are we going? I ask.

Turn right when we get to the freeway. I'll give you directions as we go.

9

Underneath the flickering streetlights, my ex-boyfriend's face looks blankly serene. I've never noticed the lines, the crow's-feet. On his left arm, I glimpse the cheap tattoo-removal scar that still spells out my maiden name.

Take this exit, he says.

We go down back roads. We speed along the boulevards. It is late and the streets are mostly empty. When my hands shake and I begin to veer, he puts his hand on the wheel and I straighten out.

Go slow, he says.

We go past the familiar places. We go past the Lucky where we used to buy eggs and cheese, where we used to play on the blood pressure machine in the back next to the pharmacy. Nearby was his old apartment, where he kept tropical birds. When he was evicted, they wouldn't let him go back in to get them. When I asked him to move in to the Husband's house, he said, That doesn't solve anything. But he came anyway.

We pass the now-closed taqueria where we first met. We were both late to meet mutual friends, and they had left before us to catch a movie. We sat down anyway. We had fish tacos. I had a pineapple Jarritos and he had a tamarind Jarritos. I had never tasted tamarind before.

After we finished, we stood outside, not knowing where to go.

Your shoes are untied, he said.

I was wearing beat-up old Nikes. He knelt down and tied my laces in elaborate knots.

When he was finished, he drew himself up to his full height awkwardly and said, Do you want to go someplace strange?

Yes.

It was a strip mall, twenty minutes down Hollywood Boulevard.

You brought me to a strip mall, I said.

It's a strip mall mosque.

A what? I looked around. It was a strip mall that had been built on the site of a former mosque. Everything of the mosque had been torn down except two thin white minarets that once rang out with calls to prayer. They stood next to a Patrón tequila billboard that read EVERYONE ELSE BROUGHT WINE. In the mall itself was a coin laundry, a bridal boutique, and a fluorescently lit Mexican bakery, where we ate lard-based pastries and cookies.

Oh my god, I lard you so much, he said from across the table, through a mouthful of cookies.

Lol, I said.

Since then, they tore down the strip mall too. It has become an empty lot behind a metal fence, and that is the lot we pass in our quiet vehicle now, on our way—I realize as he directs me in a circuitous route—to LAX airport, where he will fly somewhere, I don't know where. The minarets still preside over the space, silent.

How do I know, he once asked, if what you feel is real?

It's real, I said.

Yeah, but how do I know?

It's really real! I cracked, but he didn't say anything. I don't know, I finally said.

That was the depressingly hot summer when we were cooped up in his apartment for too long, because it cost too much to go anywhere with real AC. A biscotti costs a dollar, I said. I couldn't escape fast enough. We couldn't turn on the ceiling fan because he let his birds fly around, jaundiced and bitey. What if I dissected my feelings, pulled them apart and brutalized them so that he would know they were true? Is this enough? I'd ask. How about this? They would explode and drip over everything like bodily fluids and finally he'd be forced to look away.

If that is possible, if this is something that is possible to do, can I do it now and apply it retroactively?

Now pull up, Aaron says. Right here. Delta. That's my gate.

The sign says INTERNATIONAL DEPARTURES. I pop the trunk and he lifts out his bags. We stand at the curb, not knowing what to say. We've been broken up for seven years.

Goodbye, I say, hands at my sides.

Oh, come on. He leans in and hugs me. Goodbye. I lard you.

———

There are 99 ex-boyfriends. Then 59. Then 29. Then 9. They move out. They get jobs. They get married. Their Christmas cards fill our mailbox, along with Hanukkah and Kwanzaa cards, featuring photographs of families in matching sweater vests on Alpine ski slopes or in front of blue screen fireplaces. Even the cards eventually taper off. The remaining ex-boyfriends stay put, but sheepishly, as if they're not supposed to be here. The ones who stay, they don't really want to be found. They linger in the margins of the house; morning movies booming in the theater room, weed smoke unfurling from an unused closet.

With each and every passing year, the back wing shrinks and shrivels up, an old man's balls gradually retracting into his body.

Caleb. Chang. Charles. Chris. Cornelius. I want you all.

When I finally open up the back wing, it smells like a mildewed church basement. The AC is still running at full blast, has been running for years. I turn it off. I walk around, coughing on the dust clouds, opening windows, flipping wall switches. The light bulbs have burned out, save for a flickering kitchen ceiling light. In the living room, I empty ashtrays overflowing with years of debris: cigarette butts, a bus pass, a casino chip. I dust the empty bookshelves. In the hall closet, I find an old vacuum and begin vacuuming the bedrooms, opening the doors one by one as I go along.

It takes five minutes to vacuum a room, but there are 100

rooms. I am on door three when, through the din of the vacuum roar, I hear a sound, faint and shaky, like the tinkling of
change in a pocket. ¢ ¢¢¢ ¢¢¢.

I turn the vacuum off. It's so faint, I strain to hear it.

¢¢ ¢¢¢ ¢¢¢¢¢.

I walk around, opening up rows of doors to reveal empty
rooms, trying to follow the sound. Hello? I call out. I open up
doors four, five, and six. Nothing. I keep going. Seven, eight,
nine. It's not until door forty-nine that I find him: the Husband, sitting in an old armchair. It's been a while. Even with
his hands covering his face, I can see that he has aged, with a
lightning-bolt streak of silver in his hair. He wears a sweater
vest; he crosses his legs. When he looks up, I see that his face
is wet, is pained. ¢¢ ¢¢¢ ¢. It is the sound of delicate, fawn-like
tears streaming down his craggy mountain of a face, strewn
with white whiskers.

Head lowered, I kneel in front of him, take his moist
hands in mine.

I was calling you. Why didn't you answer? I try again.
What's wrong?

Finally, he opens his mouth. $$$.

Well, it's obviously not nothing.

$$$$$$$$$$$.

Of course I know your name.

$$$$$$. $$$$$$$$$$.

Of course I remember.

I first met the Husband on LoweredExpectations.com. He was the first guy I met after creating a profile. Under Favorite Foods I put: tacos. Under Favorite Music I put: Cat Power. I put down all the taste qualifiers that were supposed to bridge the gap between myself and someone else. Under What I'm Looking For I put: I want to know someone for longer than a few years. I want to know what that feels like. I also want not to flee. By that I mean I want constancy. I want to be constant.

On our first date, I wore suede Ferragamo pumps, several inches high, the same pair I had worn to college graduation. They were the nicest pair of anything I owned.

In his darkened, curtained apartment, he asked me to take them off. He said, Let's see how tall you really are.

You want me to take my shoes off? I asked.

It was three in the afternoon. He lived on one of the top floors of a downtown high-rise. The air was stale, as if the place had been uninhabited for long periods of time.

He held my hands as I stepped out of the Ferragamos, and I revealed myself to be very small.

$$$$$$, the Husband says now.

I oblige and look at him.

$ $$$$$ $$ $$$$$ $$$$$$$$$$$$$$$ $$$$. $$ $ $$$$ $$$$$$$$
$$$$$$$$ $$$$$ $$ $$$$ $$$ $$$$$$ $$$$ $$$$ $$ $$$$$$$$$$$
$$$$$$$ $$ $ $$$ $$$$$$$$$$$ $$$ $$ $ $$$ $$$$$ $$$ $$$$ $
$$ $$$ $$$$$$ $$$ $$ $ $$$ $$$$$$ $$$ $ $$ $$$$$ $$$$$$$$$

$$$ $$$ $$$$$$$$$. He speaks quickly, with the conviction of righteousness. The truth, when it finally hits you, sounds a lot like a slot machine hitting the jackpot.

$$$$$$! the Husband insists, grabbing my wrists. $$ $$$$ $$$$$$$$$??!!

The doorbell rings.

Is it okay if I ask you to wait? I ask him. For just a bit longer?

The doorbell rings again. I run out through the back wing to the front door.

It opens to reveal two police officers, one tall and one short.

Ma'am, we're with the LAPD, the tall officer says. He pauses. How are you this evening?

Fine. Can I help you?

We're looking for a suspect who's wanted in a domestic assault case—actually, in a string of domestic assault cases. We have reason to believe the suspect is on these premises. The short officer takes out a picture and shows it to me.

Yeah, that's Adam. He lives here, or he used to.

So, are you saying that you're housing Adam? Short looks at me carefully. What is your relation to him?

He's my ex-boyfriend. He lived here for a while. I'm not sure if he still does.

Tall pauses, licks his lips. Did he ever hit you?

Yes, I say, finally.

When did this happen?

At this point . . . I do the math, count the years. Well, at least ten years ago.

Tall and Short look at each other before, finally, Short speaks up. That exceeds the statute of limitations.

Then why did you make me tell you? I snap. An image flashes through my mind: a bloodied pillow, entombed in a suitcase, on the top shelf of the closet in my bedroom.

Ma'am, Tall says. He has priors. It's not just the cases of domestic assault, but also unlawful possession of a handgun.

I didn't know about any of this, I say, taken aback. If I'd known, I wouldn't have let him live here.

The Husband comes to the door, peeping his head out. And the children too, clad in pajamas.

What are you guys still doing up? I ask the kids. It's getting late.

The daughter rolls her eyes. Mom. It's only past ten. How old do you think we are?

These cops are looking for Adam. Have you seen him?

Yeah, I just saw him, the son says, like, just a few seconds ago. He said he was going somewhere.

I'll take care of this, I say.

Ma'am, Tall says, stepping forward. You're just going to have to let us find him.

But he's my ex-boyfriend.

Can you let us in? he asks, his foot already past the doorframe. We don't want to get a search warrant.

I hesitate. You can come in, but I'm going to find him.

The kids start running toward the back door. Wait! I shout, jogging after them.

But I know where Adam is! the son yells back. He was just here!

Ma'am! Short yells.

The kids lead the way. They're fast, champions of varsity track. They trundle through the house, gleefully jumping over sofas, ottomans, armchairs, knocking over credenzas and floor lamps.

Kids! I yell.

They punch through the door that leads to the back wing, with me following right behind. They run down the shriveled length of its hallway, opening up the remaining doors. In the distance, I hear familiar, ragged breathing. Then, a door slams.

He went outside! the daughter yells.

Outside, I pause for a second, scanning the voluminous acres of hill, most of which we own, ripe with unregulated flora and fauna. The hill bottoms out onto a freeway. It's cold. Our breath comes out in a fog.

There is a full moon. Their blond hair fans out behind them, encircling their heads like halos.

Kids! I yell again. I can hear other footfalls behind us. I don't know who is running after whom. The kids are running after him. I am running after them. The Husband is running after me. The LAPD are running after we. We are running after he.

He went over there! the son yells, veering left.

The kids go off in one direction, and despite my protests, they keep going, with the Husband, Tall, and Short not far behind. I go off in the opposite direction, intuiting something, a shape, a movement, a memory. On this side of the hill things are much harder to see. The ground is uneven, dinged with rocks and twigs and brush weed. Thorny shrubs scratch my skin. My shirt snags on a pine tree. Pebbles get caught in my sandals and cut the soles of my feet.

I think I can hear the sound of his ragged breath, but I can't be sure it isn't my own. I keep running and running. I run until I can't breathe, and I can't keep going. Fuuuuuuuuuuuuck! I scream. My vision blurs. I clutch the stitch in my side. When I blink and my vision clarifies, I see, in the distance, a single windowpane of light with a girl inside. She's standing in her kitchen in El Paraiso, barefoot in a summer dress. It's Friday night. She is going out. She is putting on her shoes, her jacket. She gazes out the window, and for a brief, implausible moment, I could swear that she is looking at me. Then she switches off the lights.

This is when I see him, standing behind a tree a few yards away. I see his body, not as big and tall as anyone would expect, but not lanky either. I see his face, still unshed of its slight baby fat. The light eyes, the dark hair. The mouth always ready to curdle into a smile, always eager to say that everything's going to be okay, always quick to promise that it'll never happen again. We are frozen, studying one another.

He breathes in steady, cautious intervals. His fingers unfurl uneasily against the bark. I know his breath as if it were my own. I know his hands, with their worn knuckles, as if they were my own.

As he steps out from behind the tree, his face passing through shadow, it is almost as if he's about to greet me, the way an old friend would after years of separation. Maybe he's going to ask me to coffee, and we'll settle all this at Starbucks. He takes one step but comes no farther, just to show that he can, and it's not until then that I realize how vulnerable I am. I am alone.

And yet.

Stop! I yell.

His face changes. He starts running again and that says everything. I charge downhill, sprinting at the fastest speed I can muster, accelerating so quickly that I can't tell if I'm running or just tumbling, if I'm falling. I don't know what I will do if I actually catch him. I can't hold him down. I can't arrest him. But I am close enough that I can see the goose bumps on the backs of his arms, and it isn't until I am this close that I realize how much I want to catch him. I really, really want to catch him. I want to masticate him with my teeth. I want to barf on him and coat him in my stinging acids. I want to unleash a million babies inside him and burden him with their upbringing.

I chase him toward the freeway, the traffic lights, cars honking, radios playing a mash of songs about heartbreak and ruin, heartbreak and memory, heartbreak and hatred, how it's the deeper intimacy.

I reach out and almost touch his shirt. I can feel the warmth of his skin, I can smell the sourness of his sweat. He jumps beyond my reach.

But I am close. I am so, so close.

Oranges

L eaving the office one evening, I saw Adam coming out of the revolving doors of the residential building across the street. He turned to the left, toward the main street. He didn't see me. I waited for a moment, giving him time to disperse into the crowd.

I thought about going in the opposite direction, picking up my train at a different stop, but then I thought, If anyone should go out of their way, it should be him, not me.

He worked in the area. The last time I saw him, he had told me he worked for a dog-care company that served wealthy downtown clients. All day he let himself in and out of their high-rise homes, picking up their heritage-breed dogs for walks and play. It'd been so long since I'd seen him that I'd just assumed his circumstances had changed, that he'd gotten a new job or moved to another city.

As I proceeded on my usual route toward the train, he

came into view again. Maybe it wasn't even him. But as we passed reflective surface after reflective surface—gleaming black SUVs, luxury storefronts—this much was clear: that was his profile, his slouchy posture, his flat-footed way of walking. The fraying hems of his jeans dragged on the sidewalk.

He stopped to linger in front of a chain clothing store, its windows showcasing faceless mannequins in wool coats brushed with fake snow. I slowed down, trying to keep a few paces between us. It didn't matter, because when he released the door handle, deciding not to enter, he looked right at me.

I froze.

He held my gaze for a second, then pivoted away, heading down the street. It took me a moment to realize that my scarf was obscuring half my face.

His obliviousness emboldened me. We passed the train station. I kept a shorter distance between us. He would become smaller and smaller, almost dropping out of my sight, and then I'd quicken my pace and catch up. Just when I'd think I'd finally lost him, he would come into view again.

The email came a few years ago. It arrived in my inbox at night. The writer identified herself as Christine, an ex-girlfriend of Adam's. They had been casual friends before dating, and then he had moved in, she wrote. After a recent incident at her home, she informed me, he had been arrested

and charged with felony domestic battery and two misde-
meanors. The email then reviewed each of the three charges,
with descriptions of what he had done. That "he strangled me
until I nearly passed out." That "he punched me in the face,
among other things." Her son had been the one to call 911.

It had been so long since I'd dated Adam, back when I was
a college sophomore and he was my supervisor at a restaurant job. The news was both revelatory and unsurprising.

Christine posed her request cautiously: Statistically speaking, it was likely that Adam had been abusive toward me as
well. It would help her case if she could collect statements
of similar experiences from previous girlfriends. "While the
statute of limitations may have tolled already on anything he
did to you, a statement regarding anything similar that was
done would be admissible in the current case as propensity
evidence." She clarified that she didn't presume to know anything that had occurred between Adam and me, but.

Had something similar happened to me?

The email then included the case number, the contact
info of the assistant state attorney assigned to the case, and
a link to a website of the county circuit clerk, where I could
find court records by doing a search for Adam's name.

I clicked the link. I searched for his name.

It took me to his arrest record, with his mug shot of
his now-bloated baby face. He was recognizable only when
I looked closely. He didn't look straight at the camera, but
slightly off-center. His light eyes were zoned out, as if he'd

willed himself out of his body. Yet he smirked, just slightly, as if he had heroically chosen to remain resistant in face of the "system."

I shadowed him into the greenish fluorescent lighting of a nearby supermarket, the kind of old-school chain that smelled of stale rotisserie. I lingered in the aisles, pretending from time to time to examine the nutrition panel on a jar of maraschino cherries, a box of kosher truffles. He moved slowly, checking and comparing prices as he collected two packs of spaghetti, some boxed crushed tomatoes, yellow onions, a seasoning bottle. He used to cook a lot of Italian dishes, I remembered.

My phone vibrated with a notification. It was this guy messaging through a dating app to confirm our meetup later that night. I had dressed nicer than usual, in a black dress underneath a twill blazer, too thin for this weather. An hour ago, I had been swiping highlighter on my cheekbones, considering how they would look in the mood lighting of a hotel bar.

I ignored the message.

At the row of checkout counters, I grabbed a box of wafer cookies so I would have something to check out. If he saw me, well, I was grocery shopping. I waited at the register next to his, where the cashier seemed to be arguing with him.

"No, it's three ninety-nine per box for the crushed tomatoes, not one ninety-nine," she said. "You want me to run your card or no?"

"Go ahead." He nodded.

"It says declined." The cashier snapped her gum. "You want to take a few items off?"

"Um, let me think."

"You can go to the back of the line while you decide."

"Take off one box of crushed tomatoes and the dried basil. Can you run it again?"

"You know, this isn't a trial-and-error process. You should know what you have to spend." It was an unnecessary thing for her to say, but he only thanked her, as if he'd heard it before. When the credit card went through, I put the cookies back and followed him out of the store.

The last time I met Adam had been after Christine first contacted me. I had hit REPLY to one of his old emails and asked if he wanted to "catch up." So a few days later, we met up. It was after work. The café was located in the back of an upscale gourmet market, and had a small seating area. The setup was cafeteria-style: you grabbed a tray and ordered at the counter.

"I'll get this," he said, when we went to check out. I had a sandwich and he had a soup. Next to the register sat a big basket of oranges. He grabbed one. "Hey, how much for an orange?" he asked the cashier. It turned out to be $2.98, which seemed like a lot for an orange. Or maybe it was perfectly reasonable.

When we found a table and sat down, his orange rolled off his tray onto the floor. We looked around, under the chairs and in the corners, but couldn't find it. He said he hadn't really wanted it. "Are you sure?" I kept saying. "They'll give you another one if you just tell them what happened."

He shrugged. "No, that's okay. I don't need it."

He had pled guilty and settled, agreeing to a sentence of thirty days. Then he'd gotten off after sixteen days for good behavior, and was currently on parole. He didn't know I knew all this. I thought he would seem different somehow. He looked the same except a bit older.

The conversation was smooth and friendly, all surface. I told him a bit about my job now, as a copy editor at a law association. He told me about dog walking, but mostly about his monied clients. He seemed to know a lot about them, their vacation homes and travels, their careers and connections. In another life, he would have made fun of these people, but now he was almost bragging about his access. I asked him if he still kept in touch with some of our former co-workers. We'd both worked at a pub-grill restaurant, where we had first met. I was a part-time server, and he had been a bartender who was also tasked with training new waitstaff. Inspired, he recounted many stories from that time. "I can't believe you still remember all this," I said.

"I have a photographic memory, don't you remember?" He was sort of teasing.

"You have very selective memory. You tend to remember people's fuckups or embarrassments." I smiled, as if I were making a joke.

"No, I remember everything. I'm an elephant." He smiled, changed the subject. "By the way, my mother says hi."

"Okay, well, tell her I say hi back."

"I took a trip home last month, and I stayed at her place. One night, some friends were over and we started playing cards. I'm not sure how your name came up, but she was just saying the most racist stuff about Asians. It was so vile, I couldn't believe it. I was like, Mom! You can't say—"

"But why would you tell me that?" I kept my voice neutral.

He shrugged. "I don't know. I mean, I just think it's interesting, the way people hide—"

"I know racism exists, that's not news." He wanted to disquiet me, I suspected, without leaving his own fingerprints.

The announcement blared that the café was closing in fifteen minutes. I had barely touched my sandwich as he finished his soup. When we returned our trays at the bin slot, he asked, "Are you going to take that home?"

"No," I said, throwing away my uneaten sandwich.

We went outside. On the sidewalk, we exchanged goodbyes. When I turned to go, he asked me if I wanted to get a drink.

He was too comfortable asking me this, I felt. "No, I should get going."

"Okay, well, good to see you again. Maybe we can get a drink next time."

"Yeah, maybe," I demurred. "Well, nice to see you."

"Hey." He touched my arm before I went. "I remember all the good times."

"Well, I remember the night you beat me."

I didn't look at him. I kept my gaze at the restaurant across the street. There were tables with couples on dates. In front of the window, a young woman passed by, carrying a gym bag that read BE THE CEO OF YOUR LIFE.

When I looked over, he was walking away.

The dream was different in that it wasn't actually a dream, but a memory that replayed in my sleep. I watched the orange disappearing off his tray, and I heard myself say, Just get another one. He shook his head, saying that it was okay, that he didn't need the orange after all. And then I would insist again. You paid for it, I'd say. You're owed an orange. He loved oranges, his favorite fruit. One of his few ways of showing care had been peeling them for me when I was sick, telling me they were vitamin dispensaries.

He resisted again, saying again that it was fine, it wasn't worth the trouble.

What trouble? But what's the worst that can happen? I asked him. So what if they don't give you another orange?

He was like that in other ways, avoidant about things that were easy to fix, anything that entailed persuading another party. He refused to call the phone company when there were unexplained surcharges on his bill. Once, sick with the flu, instead of just calling his boss, he simply didn't show up for work and forfeited his job. Back when he had a car, he was given a wrongful parking ticket (the NO PARKING signs had not yet been posted), but he avoided the ticket instead of contesting it. Because he did not contest it or pay the fee, the car was eventually booted. Again, he did nothing. Of course it was towed away. He did not reclaim it or buy another car. He just went without.

Whenever this dream visited me, in the moment before waking, I would have this burst of clarity. I would realize why he was cruel to those close to him. I would understand why he hit me.

It was almost dark outside by the time I followed Adam into the supermarket parking lot, which he cut across quickly, his plastic bag rustling. Storm clouds collected in the distance.

We crossed the concrete bridge over the river. Some of the streetlights were broken, and though I couldn't quite see the water below us, I heard the hugeness of its gulping sound, a giant trying to swallow. Then more empty lots, parking garages, big-box stores, an old diner with brown up-holstered seats, where, I suddenly remembered, we once ate. He had an affinity for diners, taquerias, counter delis—establishments of the proletariat, he extolled. But if any of those places raised their prices, he would balk and claim they had sold out, like everywhere else. "Then how does the proletariat get paid a decent wage?" I once asked.

"There are no decent wages," he'd answered, as if that settled that.

We went through a deserted, graffitied underpass, splattered with pigeon shit and feathers. There were areas sectioned off with chain-link fencing to prevent the homeless from camping out.

My scarf had unfurled from my face. There was nothing preventing him from recognizing me, if he were to turn around. If I quickened my pace, I could reach out and touch him. Just step on the back of his shoe, see what happened.

Emerging from the underpass, we crossed a trisection with broken WALK lights. On the other side of the street was a row of old, broken-down apartment buildings, and as he stopped in the doorway of a rust-colored one, I understood that this was where he lived. It surprised me, watching him fish in his pockets for keys. I didn't think it would be over so soon, although I realized we had been walking for almost two miles.

It was a three-story, multiple-unit building. The front door, with a FOR RENT sign taped to it, didn't appear to close fully. After struggling with his keys, he opened the door and disappeared inside.

It started to drizzle. On the other side of the street, there was a plexiglass bus shelter. If I took that bus, it would get me back downtown, at least. I could get to that hotel bar, if it wasn't too late.

I crossed the street and sat on the bench. I never did this, I thought. I was never here.

The ad at the bus stop was for a suburban housing development. Christine lived out in that area now. She had bought a house, and had invited me to see her. "We'll have a picnic in my backyard. I'll invite everybody involved with the case. You guys can all meet each other."

"I don't know," I said. The idea of having a get-together with Adam's exes, forming friendships on the basis of a common terrible experience, seemed too depressing. Later, I regretted not going.

Across the street, a window popped alive with light. There was Adam again, framed by the window. It was a sublevel apartment, half-underground.

He was in the kitchen, boiling water in a saucepan under a single overhead light. Though it was a messy kitchen—spice bottles in disarray all over the Formica counter—his cooking was considered and careful. It was something he felt good at, it calmed him. He took the pack of spaghetti and broke the strands in half, so they could better fit in the pot. He opened the box of crushed tomatoes and warmed it up in a separate saucepan.

The bus was coming in five minutes, according to my app.

The light of another window switched on, next to his. The first thing I noticed was the large bookcase that held rows of glowering porcelain dolls. The occupant of this adjacent apartment was a young woman who was just coming home from work. She dropped her tote bag to the floor, and then Adam came into the room. They embraced.

He picked up her tote bag and hung it on a wall hook. They sat down on the sofa. I could see their faces as they talked about their day. In their apartment, they couldn't see very far outside in the dark. Conversely, their lit window was like a cinema screen to me.

And I couldn't help myself. I jaywalked across the street. I was standing to the side of the window, voyeuring into their life. This was her apartment, I gathered, and he was living here. That was his MO. He would leech onto some girl and eventually move into her home.

All they were doing was sitting on the sofa, watching the nightly news on the TV screen.

At the commercial break, he stood up and said something, from what I could glean, about checking on the spaghetti.

Just as I turned away, he looked up at me.

———

Though it was Adam who spotted me, someone else came outside. She emerged from the back entrance, in the alley, as I was trying to walk away. It was the girl in the apartment. "Hi, I'm Beth," she said pointedly, stretching her hand toward mine.

"Hi," I said, in a not-unfriendly way. Her handshake was gentle. She wore a graphic T-shirt and a miniskirt, Doc Martens. Up close, she seemed even younger, a recent college grad.

She got to the point. "Adam says you've been following him since the grocery store."

"Actually, it's been longer than that." And, because I had nothing to hide, I added, "We used to date."

"Okay." She tried not to look surprised. "That doesn't explain why you followed him, though." She paused, and when I didn't expressly answer, she said, "I'm not sure how to ask this, but, um, what do you want?"

"I want to come inside," I said unequivocally.

She almost smiled. "And why should we let you in?"

"Why should *you* let me in," I corrected her. "It's your apartment, I'm assuming."

"It is my apartment, yes. I've been living there for the past two years."

"Mm-hmm." I nodded, as if I knew this. "So it's your decision. Not his."

"You know, I told Adam not to call the cops." It was her last-ditch effort to deter me.

"He wouldn't do that. There's still a bench warrant out for his arrest."

"A warrant for what?" Now she couldn't hide her surprise.

"For missing his last parole session." I let that sink in. "It's starting to rain," I pointed out.

Her fingers opened the door. "All right. Um, you can come in," she finally said. Then, as if making a joke she wasn't sure was a joke, she added, "Please don't do anything extreme."

I feigned indignance. "Do I look like someone who would do something extreme?"

She smiled uncertainly. "I'm not sure." But she was curious. She held the door open, and I went down the stairwell and into her apartment.

What I remember most about that night was that he called his mother right after. There were other hours to fill until the morning, as it turned out, and he was restless, with nowhere else to go except to remain at the scene of the crime, as the sky lightened through the blinds. Pacing around my bedroom, he summarized the night's events to his mother over the phone. It was late enough that the call must have interrupted her sleep. "And I hit her," he said. "And I shouldn't have done it, but." He paused, listening to the voice on the other end of the line. "No, she didn't call the cops. No, no one called the cops."

It was not the first time his mother had dealt with this,

I realized from listening in (he wouldn't let me leave the room). She was already thinking in terms of damage control. Any surprise I felt was distantly received. He had never hit me before, though he had made daily life terrible in other ways since moving in.

I told all of this to Christine, over the phone. "God, his mother. They were always fighting over something," she said. "Whenever he did something terrible, they would plot how to get him out of it."

I had met Christine in person once, at a too-formal restaurant in the middle of the day. We were both stiff and awkward, talking about everything except Adam. After the check came, she'd stood up and said, "Well, we didn't really get to talk about the elephant in the room. So why don't you give me a call sometime?" I did, a week later, and over a series of nights, we would stay rapturously on the phone with each other. I hadn't had calls like that since high school, furtive exchanges that could unfurl for hours.

It wasn't just that he was a drag to live with, I told Christine. It was that he refused to make any concessions. He didn't pick up after himself in the kitchen, leaving sprinklings of flour and seasonings all over the electric stovetop, while extolling the superiority of the gas range. He left piles of his washed laundry on my bedroom floor, which he did not fold but would pluck from as needed. He used my laptop as if it were his. He was so affronted by any minor requests, including my roommate's, to keep the living space habitable, a space for which he was not even asked to pay rent. His way of doing things was the only way, his reality was the only reality. "But I didn't see these things about him until afterward," I said.

"Neither did I. Which you can't blame yourself for, of course," Christine said. "Tell me the rest."

"The rest of what?"

"The rest of what happened that night. He called his mom, then what?" Ice clinked as she poured herself another drink.

"Well, he didn't let me leave the room. So I heard the whole phone call," I said. The details of that night were so gothic, they strained credulity.

"I don't know," he had said to his mother. His eyes had darted toward me, lying on the bed. "I don't know. She's a little bruised up. She's not, like, bleeding or anything." The lights weren't on (he wouldn't let me turn them on), so he couldn't have seen the inflicted damage, or the blood on the pillow and the sheets, the walls. He was like a little boy fudging the details to make himself look better.

I hadn't realized the extent of my injuries. My face hadn't yet started to swell, and though I felt a dull ache, much of the pain was muted by adrenaline. I knew my lip was split, and that I likely had a black eye from his punch.

He had swerved between remorse and anger as he spoke to his mother, between self-reprimands and blaming me. "I don't think so. We got into a fight. She was being unreason-

ORANGES

able. I shouldn't have done it," he had repeated, then stopped to listen. He looked at me. "She's awake. She's not sleeping. She's being very quiet."

At some point I must have drifted off to sleep.

"He did apologize," I told Christine. "At some point, after he hung up the phone, he kept saying, 'I'm so sorry.' It was as if he realized what he had done only after recapping some version of it to his mother."

"He apologized to me all the time too."

"In the morning, he bought me these little gifts," I continued. "Little apology presents." He had gone out for a walk, and came back with breakfast and a CD from the record shop.

"He stopped by the record shop?" She scoff-laughed. "What was the album?"

Exile in Guyville.

Christine exhaled. "Jesus, the irony."

"I used to listen to it all the time, afterward." It didn't make me love that album any less.

"I'm so sorry."

We didn't talk about Christine's side of things. His abusive behavior had only gotten worse over the years, was what I knew. And Christine had already told so much, to the police, to the attorneys, to his previous string of girlfriends in finding corroborating witnesses.

By the time I hung up, long past midnight, I would feel both feasted and empty. It had been years since I had thought about that time. Though I loved the sudden, hard clasp of intimacy, I would become dizzy from the divulging, the fervor of psychic bloodletting.

There would be other calls, but the intensity didn't sustain. When we spoke about our day-to-day lives, I could feel her attention drifting. Yet we were both sick of talking about Adam, about everything we had gone through. Were we processing trauma or were we simply re-experiencing it? I wondered if she did this with other ex-girlfriends she had contacted. After a few weeks, the flurry of phone conversations stopped. We corresponded via occasional texts or emails.

I turned to social media. In a series of confessional posts, I recounted what had happened with an unnamed ex-boyfriend. The outpouring of sympathy and commiseration, mostly from other women, was hot-blooded and angry. Spurred by their encouragement, I'd pontificate about misogyny, abuse survivorship, the patriarchy. Even though my hashtag-ridden posts became increasingly dogmatic and political, it didn't make what I was saying any less true. I thought of it as "owning" my narrative. But as soon as I began "owning" it publicly, my identity became flattened into this fixed thing. Being a victim was all anyone associated with me; I became a waste bin of unsolicited sympathy. Quietly, I deactivated all my accounts.

Once, I passed Christine on the street downtown. She nodded at me, and kept walking. I was not at all offended.

The one thing I never told anyone was that after my

roommate kicked him out, I would still go see him occasionally. He had found a new place to live, an apartment he shared with two others above a twenty-four-hour laundromat. I saw him there for a few months until I stopped. I would not have gone back without the presence of his younger roommates, their rooms adjacent to his down a green, fluorescently lit hallway. I would not have gone back if he had lived alone. But still, I did go back.

Though the apartment had seemed kitschy from the outside, it was actually bright and cheerful when I stepped inside. Beth liked retro, 1950s-era furnishings. Her apartment was decorated with zealous care, in the manner of a young person who believed their tastes defined them. The depressing overhead lighting was augmented by an array of tiki-themed floor lamps. Even the bookcase of dolls looked jovial, their eyes swaying at the clap of thunder. "Do people ask you about your dolls?" I said.

"Everyone thinks they're weird. But I work at a doll store," Beth said. "They look creepy but I like them." The dolls were dressed as famous historical women: Queen Elizabeth, the Virgin Mary, Emily Dickinson.

I pointed to one dressed as Frida Kahlo. "I like this one."

Adam stopped short when he came in from the kitchen. His eyes shifted from me to Beth. He said, "I thought you said you were going to talk to her."

"It's raining, and we're talking now," Beth said. To me, she said, "We're going to eat now, so. You can join us if you'd like." Despite the situation, she seemed like a proud host who wanted to show off her home.

"Thanks. I'll sit with you guys for a while." I tried to seem unassuming, benign.

He didn't look at me. He appealed to her. "That's my ex."

"I know. You didn't tell me that part." She paused, then gestured to the table. "Come on, let's sit down. We can at least talk."

I sat down. The teal Formica table was dressed with red gingham place mats. There was a serving platter of spaghetti, a wooden salad bowl, a wine bottle and glasses. An extra place setting was procured for me. "Thank you. This looks great," I said. The smell of his Italian cooking was familiar.

He stood by the table uncertainly. "Can we ask her why she followed me?" Again, he didn't address me or look at me.

"I'm here for revenge." I lifted a forkful of spaghetti to my mouth. In the silence, I added, "I'm kidding." The spaghetti tasted amazing, this fecund umami, coated in a marinara he had made with crushed tomatoes and caramelized onions, with a dusting of Parmesan and bread crumbs. "This is very good, by the way. My compliments to the chef."

This should have been enough. If this was all I'd done—caught him off guard, disrupted his dinner, discomforted him with my presence—it should have been enough.

After a moment, he sat down. He poured some wine into

a glass, and placed it next to me. "Let me know if you want any more wine."

"Thanks. That's good." To put everyone at ease, I added, "I'm not staying long." Then: "How is work?" I asked him. "How is dog walking?"

His demeanor shifted. After a moment, he replied, "I might not be doing that anymore." He took a sip of wine. "One of my clients is opening a restaurant, and she needs a bartender. I told her about my restaurant background. Could turn into a full-time gig."

"That sounds great," I said politely. "So you're going to be a mixologist."

"Yeah." Now he couldn't help himself. "It's very high-concept. She showed me a menu mock-up. The dishes are named after artists. The Rothko salmon is cooked two ways. The Jasper Johns is poached cod."

"What's the Carl Andre?"

Beth frowned. "Who's the client? Where is this restaurant?" I could have told her it was unlikely to happen.

He half answered her: "They don't have a location set yet."

I shifted the conversation. "I remember when you worked at that French bistro." It was another in a long line of restaurant gigs he held.

"It was only for a summer." He was referring to the summer he spent in my apartment. He knew I knew.

"Right. I forget why that gig ended." I was goading him now.

43

"Well, the owner didn't know what he was doing. He didn't keep the liquor stocked. I didn't have any materials to make cocktails with. I couldn't do anything except wine pours, which, really, any waiter can do." Having finished his wine now, he topped himself off. "He was putting all his resources into the food and dinner service when everyone knows drinks are more lucrative. That's a basic fact of the restaurant industry. The guy was an idiot."

He was still the same person. There was no revelation to be had, no reason to have come. I turned my attention back to the spaghetti, the cold iceberg salad.

Beth looked back and forth between Adam and me. She was almost apologetic when she broached the topic again. "So, I know this already came up earlier. But I'd like to know. You followed him here tonight. Why?"

"He has a history of abusing women," I said flatly. Before she could react, I added, "There's a documented history. It's in the court records. You can look it up."

She didn't say anything. Adam was watching us.

"You just haven't known him long enough to see it clearly," I added.

"You don't know how long I've known him." It was the first time she was defensive. She was thinking, puzzling this through. "But that's not my question." She looked at me. "I asked why did *you*—you, personally—follow him here tonight?"

"Because . . ." I faltered. "Because—I just wanted to look at him."

She waited for me to say more.

I felt childish. "Sometimes I have a hard time believing what happened to me. What he did. And seeing him again makes me realize that it happened. It actually happened."

Beth's expression was curious, a scientist studying a microbe. "And what happened to you?"

After my roommate kicked him out, the phone would ring periodically in the middle of the night, back when we still had a landline. When I picked up, a voice would say, "I miss you." If I protested, he would repeat the refrain, "I miss you, I miss you," forcing this trite, stupid sentiment on me, overriding any response. "Stop calling. I'm not interested," I'd say, but he'd just repeat the phrase over again. If I hung up, the phone would ring again and "I miss you" would grow more insistent. It would have been menacing if it wasn't also so stupid, the work of someone who couldn't think up a strategy other than a single blunt, repetitive action.

"I have a boyfriend," I finally said. Surprisingly, that stopped him. He claimed that I was lying, but then he asked for the name. "Mark Radisson." Radisson like the hotel chain, fluffy pillows and clean sheets. A convalescent state, a business conference in a midsized city. It was in the middle of the night. I was so tired. I told him the qualities of this person, about his job, and his apartment, and the things we did together, like go on drives, and walk along the lake and eat ice cream. Extremely soothing things. I spoke about Mark Radisson long after he'd hung up, and I was just talking to myself, naming things.

He never called again.

"Thank you for telling me" was all Beth said. I couldn't read her expression. It was somber. I'd like to think that she did believe me, at least momentarily.

Years later, I will look Adam up, do a search for his name online. He will end up in another town in his home state, some hundred miles away, a town with a newspaper that publishes all the arrests in the county. Within a brief time span, he will be arrested on a series of charges: for disorderly conduct, for shoplifting, and countless times for domestic violence. Into his fifties, he will be in and out of jail with increasing frequency.

Long after he moved out of Beth's apartment, long after I lost touch with Christine, the circumstances of my life changed so much I might as well be another person. I no longer work, and my time is my own. My husband, who gave me this insulated life, is away most of the day, and in the evening he doesn't want to hear my stories. He wants to live in the present. He wants to enjoy our life. It gets harder and harder to remember this earlier time.

But I do remember, with an elephant's memory, Adam's face. After I laid out his secret history to Beth, knowing that it probably wouldn't do anything, I looked at him and he looked back at me. He would win Beth back, of course, even if temporarily. She hadn't been with him long enough. And I was just a stranger, a dinner crasher. Someone who was just a storyteller. I continued as Beth's face changed, as Adam jerked away my place mat, and all the dishes and cutlery crashed to the floor, as someone protested, "But I know who he is," and then, "But people can change," just as the other said, "Leave now."

But in the moment before he persuaded her back to his side, he looked at me. I didn't know what I wanted until I saw it. It was such an open expression, a child's face. He didn't look angry or bitter or violent. Nor did he look guilty or remorseful or ashamed. He just looked trapped.

G

Without question, the best part of taking G is the beginning. The sensation of invisibility is one of floating. You walk around with a lesser gravity, a low-helium balloon the day after a birthday party. You are neither in this world nor out of it—and you could, if you wanted, just give a little jump and go rushing past rooftops, telephone wires, satellites, your ears popping, the air growing thinner and thinner, gently asphyxiating you into a soft numbness. It's a feeling that intensifies the longer you've been on it. It's not the same as being bodiless, but I imagine it comes close.

How to take G.

Step one: Determine dosage. For an average person, with a BMI between 18.5 and 24.9, one ten-milligram pill will last you about three to five hours. If your BMI is lower than 18.5, take half a dose. (If you don't know your BMI, the most reliable calculator is at cdc.gov.)

Step two: Ingest the pill with water, as you would aspirin. Don't crush it or grind it between your teeth. This is important. You want G to be absorbed slowly, so that its effects are spread out evenly.

"Okay. Let's do this," Bonnie said, handing me a pill and a small glass. "Cheers." I lifted my water in a tiny mock toast, then downed it. She watched me before swallowing hers. It takes about thirty minutes before the effects take hold. Meanwhile, you begin other preparations.

Step three: Wipe off makeup. Everyone overlooks the face, which always gives things away. Don't take shortcuts, such as overrelying on drugstore cleansing wipes. Double-cleanse, first with an oil-based cleanser, then with a water-based one.

We all had different draws to G. Bonnie's, at least initially, was something called the G-Diet, which was more effective than an eating disorder. Between the drug-induced nausea and diarrhea, the G-Diet was a surefire way to lose all your water weight, until you became a desiccated prune. Like taking birth control pills for clear skin, the side effect was the point.

Personally, it's my favorite drug. E is a distant second. My favorite sativa, Pear Bottoms, is children's cold medicine in comparison. I have done so much G that my adult sense of self formed in the complete absence of my reflection. For a person like me, that's a certain kind of freedom.

Step four: Remove clothes and personal items. I took out

my contacts, and the bobby pin in my hair. Bonnie removed her jade bracelet. Then she peeled off her tights and floral tunic. I slipped out of my blue linen dress, my skin turning to gooseflesh in the air-conditioning. As I bent forward to slide down my underwear, I could feel her gaze flickering over me for the briefest moment. Instinctively, I sucked in my stomach. Then she released me.

On my last night in New York, I visited my best friend. The train came before I could change my mind, and despite my hesitation, it didn't take that long to get from Prospect Heights to the Upper West Side. She lived in the same one-bedroom apartment we'd shared in college, in a mid-rise building between Amsterdam and Columbus.

When I reached the building, a neighbor, a retired fashion photographer, held the door for me. "Beautiful weather," he remarked, as if I still lived there.

"Like yesterday," I replied, as if it hadn't been seven years since I'd moved. I was moving again, flying out the next day to join a film studies PhD program in California. He'd once derided grad school as the vanishing point of the aimless, a now-accurate diagnosis of my situation.

I went up in the sleepy elevator to the sixth floor. Before I could knock, Bonnie opened the door. "Finally you deign to show up" were the first words she said to me. It had been a year.

"Were you just waiting by the peephole?"

She ignored my question, holding the door open in mock chivalry. "After you."

As I started to step past her, Bonnie stopped me. "Wait, you get a hug." She dragged me into her embrace, feeling my shape and size as a competitive sport. Nothing had changed. "You look thin."

"Thanks, Mom." Our Chinese mothers gauged our bodies like this, and she had become their torchbearer. Those excelling at the game are its most devout rule-enforcers. I stepped back.

"I got you a going-away present," she said.

"You didn't have to get me anything." I was wary that she was intending this night to be one of grandstanding gestures.

"You're either going to love me or kill me." She laughed.

"That sounds extreme." I took off my new clogs in the entryway. An impulse buy, they looked like loaves of bread, the kind of ugly I embraced.

I sat down on the futon that had once served as my bed. A wooden Japanese folding screen was bunched up in the corner. Unfolded, it had sectioned off the living room as my bedroom. The apartment, still smelling of shiitake bone broth, hadn't changed much since college. The mornings when we'd drink our tea together, talking even before the sun rose. The afternoons when, taking a break from coursework, we'd put on music and dance very slowly; our imaginary troupe was called Discerning Tai Chi. The night when Levi and I had a big fight, and I walked thirteen blocks in the rain and just lay down in her bed, wordless with wet clothes and hair, and she stroked my back until I fell asleep.

After graduation, Bonnie had kept the apartment. There was no reason not to. It was rent-controlled. Her commute was the same. She had continued on at Columbia, as a research assistant in the psych lab, the job she still holds.

"Here's your gift." Sitting down, she presented me with a velvet ring box.

"Is this a proposal?" I smiled, opened it. That mother-of-pearl iridescent gleam, its seashell shape, the sweet, plasticky smell. "You got G," I said blankly, my dismay eclipsed by awe that she'd managed to find it. "Wow, this is so . . . retro."

"That's right, we're gonna have a retro time tonight." Once synonymous with the early-aughts East Coast college scene, as ubiquitous as Vampire Weekend blasting at dorm parties, G has since virtually disappeared after a strict government crackdown. Sensing my hesitation, Bonnie added, teasingly, "It's your last chance."

"Are you peer-pressuring me?" I tried to stay cool.

She chanted, in a funny voice, "Peer pressure, peer pressure!"

"I don't know." It had been a long day, full of last-minute moving errands. I had dragged my mattress, embarrassingly pocked with too many stains to resell, down the stairs to the sidewalk for trash pickup. The plan had been to donate it, but it looked so intimate that I just threw it away.

"Come on. Like old times." She was serious now, but smiling hugely. There were no options, really. She knew what I was going to do.

Do you know. Do you know how easily the world yields to you when you move through it in an invisibility cocoon? No one looks at you, no one assesses you. It lifts the tiny anvil of self-consciousness. You can go anywhere, unimpeded by the microaggressions of strangers, the obligatory, waterlogged civilities of friends and acquaintances. Just go out and voyeur around, nothing but a Guston eyeball bouncing down Amsterdam, where patrons dine alfresco on a Thursday night, celebrating, already, the impending weekend.

Eager for blood, we walked along the stretch of outdoor seating, dashing water glasses off tables, upturning plates of half-eaten food, salads upon salads, to everyone's confusion and embarrassment. Petty stuff. We detoured across the street before we could give ourselves away. When G was more novel, we had been more committed and innovative. We would touch strangers discreetly, feathering down their cowlicks. We would eavesdrop on conversations, interjecting dialogue. We would float objects in the air, distorting others' fields of reality. In more destructive moods, we would just flat out damage property, fling apparel out of Urban Outfitters. We never felt guilty as long as it was a chain. We would follow people home, go up in their elevators and into their apartments. That last thing, I liked to do alone.

I could feel Bonnie's hand reaching for mine. If you're taking G with someone, it's a good idea to hold hands so that you know where the other person is, if only to tether each other to the Earth. Tonight, the sensation was headier than I'd remembered. I needed to be anchored.

On Broadway, we disappeared into the Sephora, where we spritzed the air with perfume from tester bottles. Alternating between Dior, Calvin Klein, Prada, Jo Malone, Tom Ford, we created an untenable cloud of hysterical femininity, a misting monster of jasmine, vanilla, rose, patchouli, lychee, amber, tonka bean. Customers began to leave.

When a bottle shattered on the floor, I froze. I had dropped it, releasing the grandmotherly scent of Chanel No. 5 everywhere. It had slipped right through my fingers.

"Okay, now we should go," Bonnie whispered. "How about the park?"

It was at this point that the dizziness set in. It's another side effect of G, but this time, the floor seemed to be warping beneath me. "Hey, this stuff is really strong," I said. "Does it feel different to you?"

She didn't respond for a moment, and I wondered if she was contemplating my question or if she hadn't heard me. Then she said, "It's supposed to be more extreme. Like, you know, THC levels in weed, how they're more potent? This is next-gen G."

"Next-gen. That's a thing?" I'd just assumed that what we had taken was expired supply.

"Patrick is an early investor in it."

I waited for her to say more, but she didn't. Everyone had known Patrick in college—his trust fund parties, his Supreme skateboard, which he always carried around campus but never rode. "Well, I don't feel great," I finally said.

"Okay." She squeezed my hand. "Let's get out of here."

"I think I need to lie down," I said. "Can we go back to your place? I'm sorry."

She didn't answer.

Outside, it was trash day. Bonnie kicked black bags off the curb, bursting with empty takeout containers and food wrappers and crumpled Kleenex. She was trying to keep up the mischievous mood. A car came, dragging the wet, hot garbage down the street. It was disgusting.

"Let's go to the park. Come on." Bonnie tugged my hand, and because it was my last night in New York, and because, unbeknownst to her, I didn't want to see Bonnie for a long time after this, I let myself be led.

On G, your night vision becomes sharper, more acute. I could see into apartment windows, into the lives inside: the floral arrangements, the books on the shelves, the photos on the walls. A woman sat alone at her dining table, reading and drinking a cocktail. It'd be such a relief to be older already, unburdened by the pressure to leverage your ever-fleeting beauty for whatever.

At some point, nearing Central Park, we passed Levi's former apartment. He lived in north Brooklyn now, last I'd heard. I glanced at Bonnie, but of course I couldn't see her face. Nor could she see mine.

After Levi and I broke up, on certain nights I would take G alone and, crossing the avenues, make my way over to his building. It would be late. He would buzz me in without asking who it was. Upstairs, there was a key under his doormat. Silently he would lift his comforter, and I would drag my naked body inside the warm, sweaty cave of his bed. His body odor smelled like meat drippings, which sounds disgusting, but didn't make it any less comforting. If he had acknowledged that it was me, then he would've had to chastise me for still using. So neither of us would say anything. The door would open, the covers would lift, we wouldn't speak.

He would know that it was me. He would stroke my back until I fell asleep.

In the beginning, I always took G with Bonnie. This was during the summer after freshman year, the summer we were perpetually drunk with the illusion of adulthood, though all we did was intern. Almost every night, we'd wind up in Central Park, sprawled across this giant rock, somewhere in the

Eighties. We could recognize its shape from afar, a bathing elephant. We called it the Astral Plane.

It was only on the Astral Plane that Bonnie and I would ever make out. The enormous rock, with little weedy grasses springing from its cracks, its craggy dips and indents to hold our bodies, would slowly release the heat of the day, warming our skin. I liked the way it felt, especially on the undersides of my arms, where no one knew I liked being touched.

The intimacy would get to a certain point, but no further. It felt borderline incestuous, given that we'd grown up together in the same Chinese community. Our mothers knew each other; they were friends first. I could never forget that when Bonnie pushed me to the ground. She was so light. We were considered petite by most standards, but Bonnie was thin by Chinese standards. Meaning that the differences between our bodies were only glaringly obvious in the eyes of immigrant mothers. And within China, where Bonnie would be considered acceptably thin and I would just be the funny friend. I could be Chinese thin too if I wanted. But I choose not to maintain myself that way.

Whenever we were on the Astral Plane, Bonnie would become frustrated by my noncommittal attitude toward her. She'd pin me down by my wrists, which would only make me laugh. "You and your ticklish wrists," she'd fume. She wanted to be wanted—all the time, by everyone. But, in certain moments, specifically by me. The only thing to do was to stop responding. Giving up, she'd roll off, and we'd

58

look up at the night sky, the tension never quite resolving. The leaves of the trees above us chattered like teeth. "Do you think," she asked one night, "that if they combined the two of us, we would make the perfect woman?"

"Am I lacking in some way?" I asked. "Are you?" She wouldn't stop, I thought, until she had totally consumed me. I'd end up in her digestive tract, as she metabolized my best qualities and discarded the rest.

"I don't know," she said, a little sadly. Face-to-face, Bonnie would rarely admit to feelings of inadequacy or vulnerability. But on G, she would become forthcoming about herself— a lucid, disembodied voice of compulsive disclosures.

When she was eight, she was assaulted in the stairwell of the apartment building where her family lived. This was back in Shanghai. Her family moved to the States the next year. Whether this had to do with the assault, I'm not sure. But if every day you had to pass by the same stairwell where you had been raped, maybe moving to a new country didn't seem like that dramatic a change.

We didn't meet until middle school, when our mothers became acquainted through our mutual piano teacher, somewhere in the overlap of pickups and drop-offs.

"This is the kind of girl you should be friends with," my mother informed me, enumerating Bonnie's grades; her articulate piano-playing; her delicate, ladylike bearing; her formal, old-fashioned diction, the mark of someone who had studied English abroad.

"She's not my friend type," I said. She had the coddled, prissy air of an only child from China. Which was an entire generation, more sons than daughters. At school, she got teased for her frilly, translucent ankle socks, her cartoon stationery with Chinglish phrases on them, her bone-broth breath.

My mother's face hardened. "Bonnie's not that different from you. She immigrated here when she was nine, you came when you were six," she said, as if immigration would be the only thing we'd ever talk about. All I knew was, the three-year gap made the difference between passing as American and being exposed as FOB.

Bonnie didn't have friends for other reasons. Her mother never let her leave the house except to go to school or piano lessons. I was the only visitor allowed, and only in the hour after dinner, on the pretense of doing some SAT practice exams together. More rules: We could only listen to classical music, read "classic" literature, or watch "classic" films, whatever that meant. Mostly British and American Victorian literature, and their corresponding film adaptations. Even if, within the Chinese immigrant community, the line between proactive parenting and straight-up lunacy can be blurry, most everyone acknowledged that Bonnie's mother was overzealously strict. *Even the heartiest flower can wilt from overattention* is a Chinese folk saying, probably.

I would smuggle artifacts from the outside world into Bonnie's house: *OK Computer*, *Prozac Nation*, Eve Ensler writ-

ings, early Tori Amos albums. Watching *Seinfeld* reruns, I
would try to explain to her why certain jokes were funny.
Why Americans found them funny, and why I laughed too.
Why Elaine Benes was unlike other female sitcom characters.
"She's funny without being sexualized. We're really making,
you know, strides," I would explain, so easily lumping myself
in with white women. On the SATs, I accidentally filled out
my race as Caucasian, the first and implicitly default choice.

When I had to leave, Bonnie would walk me to the end of
her driveway—the farthest point of what her mother considered the home perimeter. She couldn't go past that. "Bye," I'd
say, getting into my car, parked at the curb. "Bye," she'd say.
Her mother monitored us from the kitchen window, ready to
call her back in. Then, as if I would forget, she'd add: "Come
back tomorrow."

I knew I was lucky. I knew that I would always be able
to escape my mother, who was fundamentally more interested in herself than in her children. Which was fine, objec-
tively. Because why should a woman revise her priorities just
because she's been forced to observe the social mandate of
bearing children? The only parties who have a right to com-
plain about a mother's disinterest are her children. My twin
brother, myself. That's it. No one else.

My mother was and is beautiful. In a previous life, the one
before us, in China, she had destroyed others' relationships
with her looks, flayed men with indifferent glances, according to my aunts. Her face was almost identical to Gong Li's.

Like an actress, she was performative toward her children publicly, playing the role of a scolding mother during Chinese community events, usually church or prayer fellowship sessions.

It wasn't until I was in high school that my mother expressed any real interest in me, advising me on how I should dress, what kind of makeup to use, eating habits. She was styling me in her mold, I realized, which my brother coined as "fake natural." She tucked my hair behind my ears and warned that when I gained weight, it went to my face first. "Those are my cheekbones. Don't lose them." Her flamethrower gaze annihilated all women's magazine adages about loving yourself, all body-positivity *Oprah* episodes; it could reverse all waves of feminism. My brother got through this period unscathed, toying with his PlayStation in the basement, eating Bugles and dried squid strips. "Just fake it till you make it" was his life motto in our senior yearbook. What an idiot. He didn't even know that he was free.

The only way to separate yourself from a person like my mother is to embody her fears and insecurities about herself, to become as far removed from her idealized self-image as possible. Or, to be more specific: Go through an awkward Goth phase. Buzz all your hair off in the middle of the night, surprising her in the morning. Get a memento mori tattoo somewhere conspicuous, a reminder that the body is nothing. Put on twenty pounds and wear a tight dress. Now you're free.

The night was starting to blur. I was losing track of time. Presently, we found ourselves in Central Park. We wandered around, enjoying the bounce of the grass on the soles of our feet, avoiding the onslaught of cyclists in the pedestrian lanes, migrating toward our old haunt. Spotting the familiar enclave of trees, we embarked, for the first time in years, onto the Astral Plane. The little dips and crags in the rock still held rain from the afternoon storm, puddles in which the fruit flies and mosquitoes bred. Nevertheless, we spread ourselves across the cold, damp surface. Bonnie draped her arm around my torso, her body heat transferring to me.

"What will you do when you get to the Bay tomorrow?" she asked.

"I don't know." I thought about the plane arriving at SFO. It would be evening, still early enough to do small, quiet things, wander around and get a drink. But I didn't want to tell her even that, as if allowing her any glimpse into my new life would mar it somehow.

"You know, you could have told me earlier."

"Told you what?"

"You know what. That you're leaving. I literally found out this week."

"You know the French exit is my specialty." I kept my voice light.

"I know. You like being evasive." Now we were fighting a little bit. She sounded almost shy when she added, "Well, I'll come visit you after you're settled in."

63

I was quiet, then spoke gently. "But we live in the same city now, and we don't actually see each other that often."

"So then why did you come tonight?"

"To leave on good terms."

She scoffed. "It's like you're breaking up with me. But you're the one who never picks up. You never get back to me when I try to contact you. You're the one who's been so busy."

"You know that's not the reason." I tried not to sound hard.

When she finally spoke, it was almost inaudible: "But that was such a long time ago."

One night a few years ago, Bonnie took G and went on a solo trip through the park. At two or three in the morning, she drifted over to his apartment building. Not remembering his unit number, she pressed all the buttons on the call box until someone buzzed her in. She found the key beneath the mat of his apartment upstairs. He was already asleep by the time she slipped underneath his covers. That didn't prevent what happened, though.

This was all according to Levi, who was the one to tell me. "I thought I was dreaming," he said. "And then I thought it was you."

"When did you realize it wasn't?" I asked.

"The second time, when she materialized."

"It happened more than once?"

"I thought it was you."

I had a hard time believing that. Her body was not my body.

"I just thought you should know," he said.

When I asked Bonnie about it: "That never happened," she insisted. "When did he say this happened?" She had me repeat his account multiple times. She had hypotheses. "He must have thought . . ." I stopped listening.

"Whatever, we're all adults," I said finally, embarrassed for everyone involved.

But that wasn't even it, not really. There wasn't any defining incident that convinced me to finally stop speaking to Bonnie. More that, after college, I began to notice how she increasingly critiqued me, mostly with jabby comments about my body. If I added avocado to a salad, she would say, "Are you really going to eat that?" Unsolicited, she would tell me what her boyfriend—a German PhD student with stubby fingertips named Ulf—thought about my body. (Apparently, he had remarked on my "Margaret Cho look," which at first I thought was meant as a compliment.) Under Bonnie's gaze, I became very thin. It was gradual until it was sudden. When I went home for Christmas, my mother couldn't decide if she was pleased or alarmed.

When you play stupid games, you win stupid prizes. Like

being able to encircle your wrist with your thumb and fore-finger. Like being able to see the outline of your ribs. Like losing your period.

In the end, I blocked Bonnie from my phone, my email. I had moved out long before anyway, so it was easy to avoid her. From time to time, I would receive messages from alter-nate emails and social media accounts. "How are you?" the messages would read, as if nothing had happened. Of course, I no longer responded. Had she always had so many different online identities?

In the past year of distancing myself, I felt like a swimmer coming up for air. I worked my job as a production assistant at a film company, saw other friends, lived my surface life. I resumed a normal weight. When I looked in the mirror, I assessed that I could survive if dropped on a deserted island. I made plans for the future, applied to grad school. I learned to trust the appearance of things.

The night was getting colder. "Well, we should get back," I said, getting up. The effects were wearing off. Gaining form, Bonnie looked like a heat wave, steam billowing out of a street grate. "You're materializing."

She seemed to be studying her arm, waving it around as it gained viscosity. I checked my arm too, but there was noth-ing to see, just grass and rock. "It's weird that I'm not."

"Well, you took the larger dose."

66

"There was a larger dose?"

"There was a larger dose and a regular dose. I gave you the treat." *Bronny would think that*

"I didn't know there was a difference."

"The amount was etched on it." She said this impassively.

"You should have told me." The larger dose explained the dizziness, the shortness of breath.

"Yeah, sorry. I thought you could handle it."

"Do you know how long before it wears off? I just need to make sure that it's not noticeable before my flight tomorrow."

"Okay, well. Next time I will endeavor to make sure you're fully informed." This time, the sarcasm was undeniable. I felt oddly blank in the face of her anger. It wasn't worth fighting about on my last night in New York. I was scared, but not angry. I didn't take her seriously anymore, which I tried to hide.

"Come on," I said. "You're starting to cast shadow." It was dark enough that the streetlamps had been turned on. There was a gray tinge across the rock, a shadow of a shadow. I could see it unfurl as she stood. But the same surface didn't register any trace of me.

Bonnie's voice came at me from somewhere; I couldn't tell if she was ahead or behind. "At least we got to come here one last time," she said wistfully.

———

67

It's said that G stands for *gravity*, an allusion to the comedown heaviness, when the body feels like a stone sinking. But that's just a theory. Our old dealer, this girl in our dorm, claimed that G is short for *ghost*. She once told me, menacingly, when I bought a dozen pills, that if I took them all in one sitting, I'd turn into a ghost forever. Past the realm of invisibility is the realm of dematerializing. But it was she, after senior year, who was never seen or heard from again. No one seems to remember her name. It was Liesel.

Liesel was the one who taught me the more refined pleasures of staircasing, the semi-dangerous practice of ingesting small doses at prescribed intervals for sustained periods. I'd lie on the futon, under a poster printed with the slogan WHAT WOULD JUDITH BUTLER DO?, appreciating the low-level sensation of levitating. If you do it right, if you time your doses carefully, you can stay at sea for days.

The risk is, the longer you staircase, the longer it takes to recover, to reconcile with your body, to relearn the motions of everyday living, basic socializing. You can drift so far offshore that the swim back might seem impossible. Liesel liked to go as far out as she could, lying in her dorm room for longer and longer periods, showing up for class less frequently, missing her midterms, then finals. Her fade was so gradual that most people almost didn't notice. Once, I showed up at her dorm, knocking insistently until the door finally opened. But there was no one inside, no one that I could see.

Her missing person case was covered on a true-crime TV

show. The episode shows a photo of Liesel at a college party, a pretty, bright girl whose promising life was cut tragically short. I'm in the photo too, holding a red Solo cup and looking off frame. In the episode, I'm on camera saying hyperbolically nice things about her while looking too young to understand that I could have simply declined this "opportunity." I am labeled the "best friend" even though I told the producers we were acquaintances at best. Toward the end, I'm asked if I have any theory about what happened to Liesel, and I say, "I wonder that all the time," and look as if I'm about to cry, a token minority character in this white girl's tragic, glamorous life. The episode still plays in syndication.

Citrus helps. Squeezing a lemon into your seltzer or tea helps. Or just eating fruits whole, their pulp and seeds, drinking their juices. Levi would bring me fresh, salted pineapple juice from this vegan café near his apartment. The sun helps, absorption of heavy doses of vitamin D on exposed skin helps. Not wearing sunscreen, though unadvised by medical practitioners, helps. He would take me to the beach on weekends. We would do our studying on the shore. The consolation of dunking your head in cold ocean water after an afternoon of digesting heavy theory, the conciliatory lemon sorbet on the boardwalk after metabolizing post-structuralist critique. The winter break we drove out to the Hamptons, when he was house-sitting for family friends vacationing overseas.

If you're trying to recover after abusing G, these are some simple remedies. "But they can't do everything," Levi said. In high school, he had lost a sister to substance abuse. At first, I'd resisted his caretaking.

"But I know when to stop. I know the signs," I told him.

"What are the signs?" He was testing me.

"If my voice sounds like it's coming from underwater, I know I'm fading. So that's when I stop staircasing." I thought a bit. "And when I'm laughing, when the laughter sounds like it's being muffled with a pillow."

Chilis and peppers help, in whatever form. Hot sauce helps—shrill, vinegary tonics or sweet, syrupy srirachas. Lots of pico de gallo, with triple the jalapeño. Mexican and Szechuan cuisines help, especially after solitary, long-winter diets of yogurt and cottage cheese. Whatever gets the blood going. Whatever pushes it closer to the skin, surfacing color back into your cheeks, making you look like a real, live, flesh-and-blood person, your lips exacerbated by spices, your fingers fattened up by all the excess capsaicin. These are the signs of you coming back to yourself.

On the other side: the rich, beautiful tapestry of WASP culture that constituted Levi's life—friends playing horseshoes at backyard cocktail parties, where girls swanned in chaise longues, clinking their gin and tonics. They couldn't see me, they couldn't appreciate my double eyelid. Always, the relentless bass of hip-hop blasting in rooms of nautical-themed furnishings, faded driftwood, gingham upholstery, linen and chambray.

On the drive home from the Hamptons, Levi had other recommendations for me. "I think you've outgrown Bonnie," he said as he drove. We were in his family's convertible, the heat blasting.

It was hard to tell with him what was observation, suggestion, or directive. "Bonnie and I have known each other forever," I said simply.

"Doesn't mean you have to be friends forever."

I opened my mouth, then closed it. How to explain certain things to a white boyfriend. How to explain that I didn't have very many close Chinese friends. That, growing up among immigrant parents who pitilessly pitted the second-gen kids against one another—comparing our test scores, recital performances, college acceptances, physical appearances—my friendships with peers from that community were especially fraught. That Bonnie was the only one I kept in touch with from that time.

"You guys are actually very different," he continued. "I don't think you realize how different you are. There's something almost vampiric about her. Like the way she mimics how you act."

"Is this just because she doesn't fit in with your friends? She's not part of your *milieu*?"

He was embarrassed by any reference to his privileged

[handwritten margin note: tryant to comply against each other & bad girlfriend]

background. "Look, she still uses G, and you shouldn't hang around that."

What he was saying was common protocol; it was in all the addiction literature. You have to separate yourself from enablers. Still, I couldn't help thinking that this was really because he thought Bonnie was too FOB. If she seemed affected, it was only when he and his friends were around. Anyway, even if Levi and I fought about Bonnie, our problems weren't about her.

We drove back into the city, where he parked his family's convertible in a midtown parking garage. The sadness of returning to the city on a Sunday, of taking the subway uptown to our respective, cold apartments.

At the platform, a train pulled up. It was unexpectedly crowded, and I jammed my body through the gap in the sliding doors, forcing others to shift. "You can make it too," I told Levi, but he remained on the platform, shaking his head quietly. Why couldn't I be the type of person to wait, like him? I could feel him assessing me through the closing doors, against the mass of bodies. I watched him watching me. The train pulled away.

The timeline of my relationship with Levi: I got clean and we broke up. The dynamic had already been set—he was the caretaker and I was the patient. I'd always suspected his interest in me would end with my recovery.

"You're very beautiful," he told me later, not long before we broke up. Even as he was saying this, he thought he was

G

doing me a favor, that he was caretaking. "You should try to enhance that more."

In high school, I used to tell Bonnie the worst things about myself, teenage things. I was daring her not to be my friend. I was almost willing her to reveal my secrets to her mother, who would then tell my mother. But she'd simply say, "Is that true?"

In the upstairs den of her parents' house, she asked so many questions, inquiring about what I liked, what I thought about someone, what I wanted in the future. It doesn't take much to come into your own; all it takes is someone's gaze. It's not totally accurate to say that I felt seen. It was more that: Beheld by her, I learned how to become myself. Her interest actualized me.

b/c could articulate who I'm not → subjugating figuring it out

It was dark in Bonnie's apartment. She switched on the kitchen light. Thirsty for water, I reached for the Brita filter on the counter, but my hand went through the handle. When I grabbed the faucet, neither the hot nor cold lever responded to my touch.

"Bonnie?" I called. She was sitting headless in the dim living room. "Bonnie?" I repeated, stepping closer to the doorway. "Can you pour me some water?"

"Of course." She took a glass from the cupboard. Most of

73

her body was now visible, except for her face and extremities, like a statue of antiquity.

"Will you hold the glass up to my mouth?" I asked, and though she couldn't see me, she raised it to approximately mouth-height.

"Like this?" As I angled my lips to its rim, she gently tilted it so that a thin stream flowed out. The water fell, splashing across the kitchen tiles. I could feel it spilling through me— the shuddering sensation as if I were drunkenly peeing—but none of it was caught by my body. I got onto my knees and tried to lap up the puddle. The surface didn't even ripple. Though I could still feel, with the tiniest sense of relief, some hostile dirt on the floor.

"Bea?" Bonnie put out her arm, trying to locate me. "Bea?" She was waving her hands through the air, and her hands kept going through me.

"It's getting worse." I might have been crying, but there was no sensation of tears. "I can't feel myself."

"No, no." Bonnie was shaking her head, and as she shook, her face began materializing, revealing an expression of dismay and guilt. As soon as I saw her, I knew two things: that she had done this on purpose, and that she was at least a little bit sorry.

"I'm ghosting," I said, my breath thin, trying not to panic. "How do I stop it?"

"We'll figure it out, we'll figure it out," she repeated, almost to herself.

G

"Bonnie. How large was the dose you gave me?"

"Why don't you lie down. Lie down, lie down," she said, and directed me to the futon, her hands unsteady. I lay down, looked up at the old poster. WHAT WOULD JUDITH BUTLER DO?

I deepened and focused my breath, as they'd taught us in yoga class. I could hear Bonnie in her bedroom rummaging around, talking to herself.

I closed my eyes.

It was the sound of shoes clacking against wood floors that woke me up, and Bonnie's voice saying my name. "Bea. Be-atrice. Bea." I opened my eyes. She was standing in the doorway of the living room. Though she typically kept an Asian household, the clacking shoes on her feet were my bready clogs. "Are you still here?"

"Hi," I said. It was a gargle.

She wore a blue linen dress. It was my linen dress, sticky with sweat from my having worn it for the past two days. Most of my other clothes had been packed up.

"Are you wearing my dress?" I asked, unnecessarily. "And my shoes?" Except what came out wasn't words, only a sound like ocean waves seething against beach pebbles. As soon as I heard myself, I had the sensation of sinking. I was understanding now.

Bonnie liberated the Japanese screen from the corner,

[handwritten annotation in right margin: "are you kidding me"]

blowing dust from its hinges. She unfolded it, spreading it out to its full glory.

I opened my mouth. A babbling brook came out.

"There." She was calm now, full of resolve and peace. "Now you have your room back again." She was just addressing the futon, now opened down into my old bed, knowing I was listening.

I stared at the image on the Japanese screen. We had bought it at a resale shop, when we were looking for a basic room divider. Even when I'd lived here, I'd never really noticed the painted landscape. It was an autumnal scene: two cranes— one that had just taken off in flight, while the other looked on from a cliff—in a shower of red and yellow maple leaves.

Bonnie sat down at my bedside, like when she'd taken care of me when I was sick. It was not unpleasant. "You can live here. I'll take care of everything. I'll take care of you." She cleared her throat self-consciously. "I'm doing this for us. And I think, if you search yourself, you'll know that you want this too."

Somewhere, a person was coughing up seawater.

Bonnie smiled. The overhead light, beaming like a halo around her, seemed to intensify. "Do you know how long I've wanted to do this?" She was so bright and clear, so certain and lucid. It was conveyed by her eyes, virtually identical to mine.

After another moment, she pressed, "Do you want this too?"

I used my last words to speak. "I do."

76

Yeti Lovemaking

M aking love with a yeti is difficult and painful at first, but easy once you've done it more than thirty times. Then it's like riding a bike. The human body learns. It adapts. The skin toughens, capillaries become less prone to breakage. Contusions heal by morning—you don't even see them. Certain fluids stop secreting altogether.

And you don't call it making love, because it's not the same. I could tell you the name of it, but there is no known phonetic transcription. The name of it is a mating call. First the yeti calls, and then you call, and that's the name. That's how the act is initiated. It takes two parties to make the sound of the name of the thing that you're going to do. Which is different every time. Which grows stranger and more lonely every time.

You have probably heard the call so many times, walking

through the parking garage of your office building, in this palatial lakeside city where women are always in congress with mythical creatures, unbeknownst to you, under your nose. Maybe you thought it was a foghorn, even though it was a clear night. Maybe you thought it was wounded coyotes wandering, again, downtown. Or someone grieving, the same way every night, boring, almost, in her distress. But I was not grieving.

I met the yeti three months after we broke up. It was at the wine bar near the ad firm where I worked, where you occasionally waited for me that summer. A man in a gray suit and glasses came up. He was a businessman, this man, or had the accoutrements of one.

He bought me a cocktail without asking, and proceeded to explain, casually, that he lived in this neighborhood, just a few blocks away. Actually, what he said was six blocks. No, five and a half blocks. That's what he said, five and a half blocks, as if he were afraid that at six blocks I would say no. I didn't tell him that actually, I liked him up to eight blocks. In our city, that equals a mile. I liked him up to a mile.

My friend told me not to go, but I went anyway. "You don't know if he's a serial killer," she said.

"Normal people have one-night stands too," I said, tossing back the cocktail that I hoped was spiked with Spanish fly. It was a Manhattan.

We walked the five and a half blocks. The city was so beautiful at night, full of glistening neon and terra-cotta. I walked by everything that looked familiar, all the glossy bars and restaurants and shops I'd frequented over the past ten years. It doesn't take much to convince yourself that you're doing okay, just some discretionary income and a regularity to your days. When I wake up in the morning, I make myself coffee in a French press. Next to my cup and saucer, I put a small spoon on top of a linen napkin, folded diagonally. It's like my favorite thing. I thought about this on the walk over to his apartment.

The large brick building he lived in was landmarked. Its Otis elevator groaned. It was then, not fifteen minutes after we arrived at his sawdust-scented loft, that he revealed himself. I don't mean that he took off his pants, though he did that too. What he did was, he gave me a glass of water. And by the time I finished it, his human suit lay crumpled on the floor, cleaved in two by a zipper seam, to reveal a shiny, sweat-dampened abominable snowman. A thunderous sound filled the room. I thought it was my heart, but it was him. He was panting furiously, newly emerged from his compact, human-sized cocoon. This gave me the impression that I could outrun him.

"You tricked me," I said. I was sitting on his sofa, a Crate & Barrel piece, the Silhouette model upholstered in boiled wool dyed a shade called English Moss. I knew this because I had named the model and I had named all the upholstery options. (You asked me once what a marketing copywriter does. "I create narratives for furniture," I said.)

The yeti sat down next to me. "Not making any sudden moves," he said, holding his paws up in mock surrender. He located an ashtray before lighting a cigarette. "Sorry, did you want one?" He smoked American Spirit lights.

"No, it's okay." Making conversation had become a delicate art. "Doesn't it get hot in the summer?"

"Always." His laugh was surprisingly high-pitched. He'd probably been asked that so many times. He handed me a pamphlet and wandered to the bathroom. "I'll give you some time to read." I heard water running, and something that smelled like Old Spice wafted through the air.

The pamphlet, sponsored by the Center for Yeti Well-Being, was titled, "Yeti Interaction and Appropriate Engagement." The first page opened with a quote by the ecologist Robert Michael Pyle: "We have this need for some larger-than-life creature." The rest of it explained the history and culture of the yeti. It explained my options.

The yeti came from the Himalayas. In the face of human overpopulation, entire clans had migrated to the farthest reaches of nature, to its highest, least hospitable altitudes. Only since the 1970s had they descended and learned to assimilate into human society. While there had been reported incidents of humans being eaten, those cases were considered anomalies, as the yeti diet was primarily plant-based. The yeti population stood at an estimated 19,300. If I was reading this now, I was lucky enough to behold this mythological creature, whose lineage stretched further back than my own. Fate had found me. The plural of *yeti* is *yetis*.

When I looked up, he was leaning against the doorframe, sipping a glass of water. Brigitte Bardot on a bearskin rug. Sophia Loren in an enormous mink coat. The yeti smiled. "This is not a dream," he said. He was 174 years old. He molted twice a year.

The first time you came over, you brought a handful of scarlet cockscomb. You explained how to dry the flowers, how to bind them and hang them upside down in a cool place for two to three days. "The thing about cockscomb is that it retains its color after being dried," you said. "It should begin to expel a shower of black seeds after the first day," you said. I laughed. I looked at your eyes and thick, curly auburn hair.

"Are you Jewish?" I asked, from beneath you, where all the jagged rocks were.

"No, the opposite," you said. You had descended from a long, exhausting Germanic line. It included butchers, welders, metalworkers, and, at the tail end, two fragile writers: you, your father. You taught literature at a community college, and in the summers worked as a bike messenger.

I remember it rained a lot that summer. And you worked a lot too. You were thin from biking around all day; your protruding clavicles collected rainwater.

I closed the pamphlet, pretending to have finished. The yeti made his approach. "Do you want to pet my fur?" he asked, almost shyly. His camel-colored fur, drying by street-light, looked luxurious.

He crossed the room, slowly, and knelt in front of me. I touched both his shoulders, as if knighting him. It was soft. I hadn't thought it would be this soft. It was like petting a Maine coon times ten. And when I heard the growl emanate from him, I wasn't scared, because it wasn't predatory—it was a growl of pleasure. It was a purr uttered by someone who wasn't used to purring, so it came out harsh and strangled. This city was not his natural habitat.

Only later would I understand that a yeti asking you to pet his fur was the ultimate privilege, that we were already bonding. When I drew my hand back, there was blood on my fingertips. His skin was surprisingly scratchy.

"I didn't know this was going to happen," I said.

"It's in the pamphlet," he said.

The last page of the pamphlet, titled "Yeti Lovemaking," explained the differences between the human body and the yeti body, differences so significant that strict compromises had to be brokered before this unnatural act could proceed. The yeti epidermis was lined with tiny incisors, and had been this way for millennia. Meanwhile, the human body had evolved. The human body learned. It adapted. The yeti body survived by the opposing principle: by not evolving. The yeti body does not yield. It is not at all yielding.

"We're like cockroaches," the yeti joked. He was reading

over my shoulder things he already knew by heart. "But this doesn't really give the full picture of yeti lovemaking." He explained that once he'd expunged his cloud of pheromones, I would go into another mind state altogether. First would come blindness, the formation of saline crystals in my eyes, then a blood thickening that would feel like a headache, but a really good headache. A rash would spread across my skin, the upper torso area mostly, blighting it with red clouds. It was a chemical thing. The effects would last about four hours.

I looked at my cell phone. It was 9:37 p.m. In four hours it would be 1:37 a.m. Few buses ran that late.

The yeti looked at me as I contemplated this. He said, "But that's kind of a shitty thing to do to someone without telling them first. I don't want to start anything unless you want to." From the way he said this, I could tell that he had made mistakes in the past.

"Would I turn into a yeti too?" I asked.

"I'm not a vampire."

I blushed.

He paused, wanting to broaden the point. "Do you know what it's like to have to hide your true nature at all times?"

We looked down at the blood on my fingertips. I was sweating. This was because his pheromones had begun to secrete—just a bit, he couldn't help it—and I was beginning to feel their effects. Cars honked outside. Women sat at sidewalk cafés with their financier boyfriends, eating late-night

Nicoise salad. Only their hands looked old. The lake kept rolling. Weatherman Tom Skilling said it was going to storm that night. I wondered if I had closed the windows in my apartment. "I never gave you my heart," you told me, two days before you got into that bike accident, breaking three ribs and your ancient, Germanic clavicles. If your body had been broken beyond repair, I would have paid them to pluck out those bones for me—me before all others: friends, family. It had been raining that day too. Whatever I felt, whatever this feeling was inside of me, there is no place for it. There is no place for it to go, and I would have to carry it around inside of me for a long time, so long that it would fossilize and become a part of me.

The silence in the yeti's apartment deepened. I wandered over to his record collection, past his mantel displaying mid-century lighters, past his closet filled with trench coats and shoehorns, past his credenza stacked with pamphlets. "You have a great selection," I said.

"Thank you." He crossed his legs and lit another cigarette. Yetis are the last real men around, I thought. Everyone else just reads men's magazines. "What do you want to hear?"

"A sad song with a good beat." I ran my finger across the spines. I put on Janet Jackson, *The Velvet Rope*.

I turned around.

"Okay," I said.

When the yeti initiated the mating call, it was familiar and low, an oceanic bass line that churned up seabeds, that could've impregnated whole orca whales if it'd tried. His call lasted for about a minute, and then it was my turn.

My call was different from the yeti's, but it reflected his; they were two halves of a whole. My call was a shriek down a hall of mirrors, riddled with buckles and clasps and nooses. It pierced through the city, through concrete and glass, obliterating insects, parching the throats of bystanders, before finally hitting a cruising frequency that only yetis, only you and only I, could hear.

That was the call you heard, the one that made you pick up the phone, not the next morning or the following weekend, but months later. During that time, I had turned another age. Fall had passed into winter. It had been snowing outside, and all I wanted to do was moisturize and drink water next to the radiator.

"I had a dream about you" was the first thing you said. I didn't say anything. So you began to describe it, the dream, and I began to listen. It was nice, modest in scale but not in feeling. I was in it, you were in it, other girls were in it. Rife with Hitchcockian motifs. Set against a western backdrop. It contained things that maybe at one point I'd waited to hear, but in the waiting had grown distant and oblique. And when you were finished, you waited.

On the other end of the line, I tried to speak. Broken vocal cords tried to strike, but it was like wet flint against steel. What came out was a raptor rasp, what came out were shiny metal clicks.

"Hello," you said. "Hello."

I waited for you to hang up, but you remained on the line. Outside, the snow fell in blizzarding droves, quietly obliterating the sidewalks, the buildings, the city. Your voice got soft. It sprouted nightshade. "Listen," you said. "Don't hang up. Just listen."

Returning

When I awoke, it was to a near-empty plane. Someone was shaking my shoulder. "Yes, sorry," I murmured, eyes fluttering open. "Sorry, so sorry."

"You wake," the flight attendant commanded me.

Then I stood up too quickly, as if I were late for school, grabbing my shoulder bag from underneath the seat. The other passengers had left. It was unlike Peter to leave me floundering like this, disorientedly wiping sleep crumbs from my eyes in front of some stranger. And yet.

"You forget anything?" the flight attendant asked. "Check."

I peered into the overhead bin. At least he had taken our carry-on luggage. "I think that's it. Thank you," I said to the flight attendant, whose name tag read AMINA.

"Good." She nodded, and allowed me past.

The last thing I remembered was her demonstration of putting on an oxygen mask in case of emergency. Standing in front of the curtain divider separating Economy from First Class, she had mimed disaster protocol. In case of an ocean landing, the seat cushion could be used as a flotation device. I had closed my eyes then. In case of a crash, I thought, as the Ambien took effect, my husband would put the oxygen mask on me. He would inflate my seat cushion for me. We'd reconcile our marriage in the face of catastrophe.

I disembarked from the plane. Peter was not at the exit either. A welcome sign, printed in English, greeted all arriving travelers: THERE ARE NO STRANGERS IN GARBOZA.

The only airport in Garboza was small and outdated, a cement-gray block of Communist architecture. The signs around me—denoting baggage claim, restrooms, et cetera—were written in Cyrillic-like Garbanese. But what struck me was the absence of identifiable brands. No Starbucks, no Hudson News, no duty-free shops with cartons of YSL cigarettes, Davidoff perfume. The dusty café next to the boarding gate did not even have a sign for its name. And there were no visible advertisements, no neon, no lit-up signs. Not even background Muzak. Just the hum of the fluorescent lighting.

It was a small place, we would find each other soon enough. I walked around the airport, scanning the scattered crowds. It was my first time in my husband's home country.

Through the large windows, past the river that bounded the airport, you could see the town on the hill. This was the

capital of Garboza, also called Garboza. So Garboza, Garboza. Disembarked passengers were already crossing the
bridge with their rolling luggage. It was close enough that
you could hear church bells ringing. And see little red flags
waving in the wind, a field speckled with sheep, and the forest
bordering it to the east. Once, in front of a Brueghel painting
at a museum, Peter had crumpled his hand over his face like a
napkin, and wept so uncontrollably that a guard had ushered
us out of the museum, not even allowing him the dignity of
a restroom visit.

Standing in front of the airport window, I understood
with the lucidity of the just-awoken: Garboza looked like a
Brueghel painting.

There was a line outside the men's restroom. I didn't see
Peter there either. Going farther: a restaurant with a mural
of the sea, an unattended shoeshine station, a currency exchange, and a travelers' shop. The shop sold a random as-
sortment of merchandise: shoelaces; off-brand "Duracogg"
batteries; various nuts and dried fruits in sandwich bags, as if
someone's mother had packed them; lumpy travel neck pillows filled with beans or grain, sewn up with Garbanese folk
textiles.

When I reached the customs area, I circled back. Our passports and visas were in our carry-on, which Peter had taken.
He would not have gone through customs without me.

I returned to the gate, went back to the airline service
counter. There, I asked the attendant, whose name tag read

serk, for assistance. I told him my name. "I can't find my husband. We just got off the same flight. Maybe you could use your intercom and call him to meet me here?"

"That is unusual." Serk regarded me warily, his silver-streaked eyebrows knitting together in skepticism. "Are you from Garboza?"

It was such an odd thing to ask, since I didn't look remotely Garbanese. I thought it was an unsubtle maneuver calibrated to reveal my ethnicity. "I'm American," I said, and before he could ask me where my parents were from, I added, "But my husband, he was born in Garboza. He's Garbozan American." I hoped this would legitimize my request.

Serk nodded. "What is his name?" When I told him, he smiled, as if everything made sense. "Ah. Then name is not Peter. It is Petru. That is true Garbanese name."

"Yes, he goes by that sometimes. But the name on his American passport is Peter." I seemed to be arguing.

"Here, he is Petru." Serk glanced at the computer for a moment. "You travel here for Morning Festival?"

"Yes. I'm looking forward to it." I smiled agreeably.

"Ah. We used to have visitors from around the world, especially Americans. That's why we all learned English. Now it's just Garbanese who go to festival. We receive so few tourists nowadays. You are brave to come." He looked distractedly at the computer, perhaps confirming something.

"What do you mean that I'm—"

"Okay," he interrupted, still looking at the computer. "I

will announce over speaker for husband to meet you. You go to café. I tell him to meet you." He gestured to the café next to the gate, presumably the designated waiting spot. "We will solve mystery of missing husband."

He had been working a lot. As a result, I was alone a lot. Hard to say if I was lonely; just that, freed from chores like preparing dinner, I was surprised by the open expanse of time. Not only surprised, but embarrassed by the domestic tasks that would otherwise have filled it: the procuring and preparation of organic produce and proteins to make culturally indeterminate dishes like salmon-broccoli-quinoa bowls—all of that seemed, suddenly, like marital pageantry. Except no one was watching. In the time freed up by not cooking, I was supposed to be writing.

By myself, I didn't want or need that much: chips and hummus, maybe, berries and yogurt or something. Two things make a meal. Three things make a cocktail. By myself, I had at least one vodka soda with lime every night; the second one I would put in a thermos and drink as I walked around the neighborhood tipsily. It was a way of putting myself to sleep.

On one of those nights when I was alone, I took a long walk to an informal college reunion. It was taking place at someone's home, more of a small gathering of friends and acquaintances. The route was bisected by a river. I walked through unfamiliar neighborhoods west of the water, passing the ungroomed, swampy riverbank with docked tugboats, a poultry shop that sold live chickens killed on-site, the shaggy, weed-filled parks, the hot-pink and lime-green facades of Mexican paleterias, a Polish furniture showroom of mostly pleather bachelor sofas, the gold-leafed, columned facade of the Cambodian Community Center, and countless Eastern European taverns.

I arrived at a modest bungalow-style house with a shaggy fir tree whose unkempt branches I had to brush aside to ring the doorbell.

"If you wouldn't mind taking off your shoes" was the first thing Y had said to me since graduation. It was his house, I assumed. I didn't know him that well, though in college, we'd circulated in the same friend groups, been to the same parties.

"Of course." I slipped off my boots. In the living room, a dozen or so guests milled around, nibbling on canapés off paper plates. No one looked immediately familiar. The friend who'd invited me hadn't come yet. A baby was crying. I guess I'd expected a different type of party, but given that we were in our mid-thirties, I shouldn't have been surprised by all the children and spouses.

From the din of the conversation, it sounded like people were updating one another on their careers, their new homes. I would make the rounds, I decided, show my face like a clean handkerchief, then leave.

Next to me, a toddler made his way toward an end table, where sat a cup of orange juice. I held out the cup to him, but he waddled frustratedly in place, unable to inch closer. The mother came over, telling him, "I told you, don't run off without asking me." He was on a leash, I realized. The grosgrain strap was wrapped around her hand.

"I think he just wants some juice," I said, showing her the cup.

She wrinkled her nose. "That's not juice, it's a cocktail. I can smell it from here."

"Oh, sorry." I felt implicated. "It's not mine. I'll dump this out."

"Here, I'll take care of it." It was Y. He had come from behind, and took the cup from my hand.

"See, this is why you can't run around by yourself," the mother was telling her kid, who dragged on her skirt in protest. She looked at me. "Do you have kids?"

"No. My husband wants at least one, though."

"And you as well, I presume?" She was smiling.

"Well, at the moment we're just focusing on buying a home," I said, as if the two were interchangeable.

She nodded, understanding what I was saying better than I did, the linear narrative of marriage, house, baby. "Enjoy this time."

"Thanks." Not knowing what else to say.

In the kitchen, Y offered to make me something, and, sitting down at the counter, I told him to surprise me. He poured a few ingredients into a doubles glass, took a knife to an orange. A drink materialized in front of me.

"It's a negroni." He hesitated. "You liked it in college."

"I did?" I took a sip. It was citrusy and a bit too sweet. "This seems like something I would've liked in college," I said, unsure if I was lying. It was likely he had confused me with Bethany Wu, the only other Asian student who'd majored in comparative lit. It had happened a lot back then.

"No?" He noticed my ambivalent expression.

"It's nice to be reminded," I said delicately. What did it matter if he had mixed me up with someone else, if I was the one enjoying it now?

He studied me for a moment. "Someone told me you're a writer."

"I had a novel out a few years back." Maybe he hadn't mistaken me. "But I haven't been writing much lately. I'm more of a 'housewife' now," I said, making hideous air quotes. I didn't know why I was doing this, preemptively dumping on someone's expectations.

"Ah, okay," he said, politely retracting. "Well, I'll check it out."

"Thanks." The only position to assume is the position of gratitude. I changed the subject. "A lot of families here tonight. This is maybe the first party I've been to where people are bringing their kids."

"I guess we're all at a certain life stage," he said, a little disinterestedly. "Not to generalize. I still live here alone. Probably always will."

I looked around at his bare kitchen, the scuffed floor tiles. "It's a lovely house."

"It's gotten a lot of wear," he said, cutting through my nicety. Realizing his curtness, he added, "I work from home, so I'm pretty much here all the time."

"What do you do from home all day?"

"I'm a writer too, sort of." He explained that he worked as a cartoonist, had published a graphic novel under a pen name. "It came out five years ago."

"Maybe I've seen it somewhere?" I waited for him to specify the title.

"Yeah, maybe." He sipped his drink, and left it at that. I remembered how, as an undergrad, I had always been vaguely annoyed by Y. He was always just kind of standing there, not making any social gestures. How was he so special that he didn't have to work to justify his existence? I'd wonder. I was constantly overcompensating back then.

I set the glass down. "I'm going to wander around your house, if that's okay."

"Yeah, of course."

I walked up the staircase. The upstairs held a bedroom and a study, either empty or sparsely furnished. The living room was the only fully decorated room in the house. Which was the affectation: the living room or the rest of the house?

In the study, one shelf held multiple copies of a single graphic novel, *Arrival Fallacy*. Paging through the first few pages, the thin, shaky, melancholic line looked totally familiar. I had read it before. In all those years, I'd never known that Y was the author.

I put the book back on the shelf. I had a copy at home.

When I returned downstairs, more guests had arrived in the living room. I still didn't see my friend. Y had also migrated to where all the guests clustered, but he didn't seem to be socializing. He was still just kind of standing there. It hit me differently this time. What I'd mistaken for snobbery was a kind of self-acceptance. Unlike the rest of us, he didn't swim against the tide of himself.

He caught my eye, and I gave a small wave goodbye. Quietly, I slipped outside.

Peter wouldn't be home yet by the time I got back. In preparation for home buying, he was teaching an extra evening class about fiction and memoir, called Truths and Half Truths. They discussed autobiography and autobiographical fiction, the shaded differences. I knew his schtick. First, he would bring up the topic of alternate selves, talk about fiction's capacity for stretching memoir, for deepening autobiography.

"Fiction can be a space for the alternate self," he would tell them, drawing an iceberg on the dry-erase board, its above-water shape and its underwater enormity. "It often serves as a fantasy space for our other selves." Actually, he'd say "subliminal space." He was the kind of teacher that students fell for because he gave the impression of intense listening, the warmth of being beheld. *[handwritten: fel that he cars abt what they have to say]*

When I returned to our apartment, its surfaces messy with clutter and crumbs, I brushed my teeth and washed my face and applied some facial compounds. I found my copy of *Arrival Fallacy*. I made a cup of tie guan yin tea, which I drank slowly in bed as I flipped through the pages, trying to remember the ending.

The headlights of passing cars spraying across the walls and ceiling put me to sleep.

"Just pretend I'm not here," my husband said later, sliding underneath the floral covers, attempting not to wake me. I could smell the construction site he had walked past, its chalky scent. The neighborhood was full of landmarked, early-twentieth-century churches and schools that were fast being converted into luxury condos.

When we were first married, I became freakishly devoted to being a good housewife. It was like playing house. I woke up before him just to make coffee. I bought fresh flowers every week. I researched the toxicity levels and biodegradability of various household products. I made varieties of salad dressing from scratch, even though we were both immigrants from places that considered eating raw vegetables primitive. I scrubbed imaginary grime from between the bathroom tiles.

And washed the dishes by hand instead of by dishwasher because it gave me a strange, dutiful pleasure, the scalding water on my skin in the dead of winter, and the expensive hand cream I applied afterward.

He never made me do these things, or expected me to. The pressure came from within.

pressure to be a housewife is internalized

Arrival Fallacy chronicles a space crew's return to Earth after a successful mission. They have identified an elusive twin planet, almost identical to their own except untouched by civilization, replete with natural resources. This finding is expected to pave the way for humans, greatly diminished in population after economic and climate crises, to begin the process of colonizing it.

Upon their return, the crew discovers that the private company that had employed them has folded after bankruptcy, and with that, all records of their mission have been lost. They have been on their mission for almost two hundred Earth years. No one is expecting them, and their wives and children have long since passed. Though their vessel is tentatively received by an aeronautical arm of the government, they are treated with suspicion. After hearing their story, one official finally asks, in exasperation, "Who asked you to do this? What made you even want to take on this responsibility?"

———

Over the airport's speakers, I heard Peter's name being called in a garble of Garbanese. Would he know to respond to Petru? Would he come back for that? As the announcement went on, the words became fuzzed with static, and the sound system seemed to break.

At the café counter, I ordered obsequiously, pointing to a cake with red fruit filling and a slice of pink Jell-O. I then picked a tea bag from a glass jar at the register, one that looked like chamomile.

With my tray, I sat down at a table closest to the large window. I felt someone sit next to me. "What took you so long?" When I looked over, I saw it was a woman. "Oh, I'm sorry."

It was the flight attendant from earlier. Amina. She looked like a different person, having loosened her bun, taken off her eye makeup. She asked, "You are still waiting for husband?"

"I've walked around the airport and haven't seen him yet." I shifted register, tried to make small talk. "He was born in Garboza, my husband. He lived here as a child. But it's my first time here."

"He is here or not here. It is small airport," she said, cutting shrewdly into a meat pie that squirted a yellow oil.

"He's here." Was it her unsolicited counsel or my defensive response that irritated me? "We're attending the Morning Festival tonight."

She took a bite of the pie and chewed for so long that I

wondered if she'd even heard. Finally, she said, "In Garbanese, the word *morning* also means *night*. It's the same word. So Morning Festival could be called Night Festival."

"Oh, okay. I always wondered why the Morning Festival takes place at night." I smiled politely, then sipped my tea, which was not chamomile. It had a smoky, hay-like scent.

"It's both morning and night! The burials take place at night, and the uncoverings happen in the morning." She tsked. "Your husband tells you nothing about Garboza?"

"He didn't say anything about burials or uncoverings," I said, a hapless American. There was a festival at night, Peter had told me, during which participants wrote resolutions for themselves on slips of paper, then threw those into a bonfire, which was later doused with holy water. By morning, if a person was lucky, the resolution would come true, and they would be improved in some way. That was all I knew. "I'm told that it's a festival about transformation."

"You're *buried*," she emphasized. "You're buried overnight in the forest, and in the morning, they uncover you. They dig you up. If you're lucky, you will, as you say, transform."

"Oh, wow." I took a sip of tea, unsure. "Have you experienced this yourself?"

"If you're sick and you have no choices," Amina continued, ignoring my question, "then you do it. My aunt was, as you say, depressed, and then she attended Morning Festival. She felt better after that. It didn't make her happy, but she could get out of bed and work, cook, take care of children. You know, normal things." She looked at me. "So, what is wrong with you? What do you fix?"

I shifted. "Well, I'm sure everyone has something that they wish they could—"

"You have to be specific or it won't work." Amina's attention diverted back to her plate, as she cut up the remainder of the meat pie. "The problem is," she continued, "not everyone survives by morning. My cousin, she lost arm in a farm accident. The arm, it grew back, but she herself did not survive." She glanced over at the untouched items on my tray. "You're not eating."

I took a bite of the pink suspended-fruit Jell-O slice, which turned out to be some kind of head cheese. I pretended not to be flustered. She watched me as I chewed on unbidden animal parts. When I swallowed, she looked away, out the window.

"Your husband! That is your husband, no?" she asked, pointing.

And, looking at the river, I saw him. Or, I saw his back. But it was unmistakably him. He was walking across the bridge, dragging our rolling carry-on, headed toward the town.

I ran up to the window. "Peter!" I yelled. "Peter!"

"He can't hear you," Amina said.

But the amazing thing was, he could. Or so it seemed. He hesitated, stopped, and then he looked back toward the airport. He was close enough that I could recognize it was him, but far enough away that I couldn't decipher the expression on his face.

He paused for a second, then turned and continued toward his home village.

I met Peter on the promotion circuit during the year our first novels came out. An entire ecosystem of bookstore readings, literary festivals, writers' conferences, campus visits, awards ceremonies, and author after-parties opened up before us. At a lit festival, we were cast on the same panel on immigrant writers, though our novels were about vastly different topics. Onstage, we were all lined up in a row, as if in front of a firing squad. This sense was somewhat alleviated by the presence of a conference table, adorned with elegant drinking glasses. When I tried to pour myself water, I found that the pitcher was empty, had never been filled. The setup was strictly ornamental.

The host prompted us to introduce ourselves. "Just to begin, I'd love to go down the row and have each of you talk a bit about the way the past figures in your novel. We'll start with this end and move down the row."

The writer beside me spoke. "My novel, *Homecoming*, moves from reality to fantasy. I gave my protagonist everything he secretly wanted. He idealizes his past in his homeland. And so, when he returns, I put everything back the way he remembered. Of course, it becomes nightmarish for him. Because there is no such thing as a real return." *[handwritten: so like, what his doing now?]*

Peter was the unofficial star of the panel, which was loosely titled after his novel, I realized. The novel was already a bestseller. The reviews, which unfailingly noted his hefty advance, framed *Homecoming* as an allegorical tale about fleeing fascist regimes, touching on themes of memory and immigration. The messaging seemed both vague yet overdetermined, pushed by marketing. My impression was that the book was extremely legible but not that interesting. Not that I'd read it.

In his glasses and a button-up shirt, he held himself very still in front of the audience and spoke with a gravitas that could have made anything sound true. I was wary of writers like that. Under the table, however, his hands were clumsy barnacles, clammy and heavy-knuckled, mouth breathers of hands. When he noticed me looking, he winked, a gesture almost imperceptible to anyone else, an actor breaking character. *[handwritten: so is the real him from the start too]*

It was my turn next. "My book is about this couple who spend a lot of time and resources planning for this idealized future, which never comes." I paused, losing the thread. "Um, so they make a big, life-changing decision based on this fantasy of how great the future is going to be. But then the wife breaks out of the spell, but the husband doesn't. They become separated on different timelines." *[handwritten: so that kinda like this too]*

Whereas I was hesitant and slow-moving, robotic in front of the crowd.

On the book-promotion circuit, I felt like the executor of a modest estate, interpreting and acting upon the intentions of the deceased, reanimating her process of writing, retracing her thoughts, presenting publicly on her behalf. Because I bore her likeness. Because I inhabited her body, from which in the mornings a soft keening sound emanated, and then, in the afternoons, disconsolate bouts of weeping, before I washed my face and then, with imprecise concealer, over-corrected the skin under my eyes. The only position to assume is the position of gratitude. → repitition

I had begun writing my novel when I was in my twenties, and by the time it was published, I was in my mid-thirties. The person who entered the dream was not the same one who awoke from it. I had overslept, only to find that, in the interim, friends had moved to the suburbs, had begun families. Their lives had progressed while my life had been frozen, was just now thawing.

That was the year I gave myself over to superstitious behavior. I vaped ritualistically, before and after each event. I dressed only in charcoal gray, navy, and black, as if to obscure myself in dull, drab colors. And I doused myself in lavender, dripping essential oil on my shirt sleeves, on hotel bedsheets. I drank a cup of lavender tea every day, though I disliked the bitter aftertaste. I wasn't sure where these compulsive rules came from, whether they were ad hoc protection spells or symptomatic of a stress-induced type of OCD. But I enacted them for a long time, long after anyone was looking or interested.

Another self was needed to move into the future.

After the panel, a group of the authors ended up at Peter's apartment. We drank wine and took turns playing records for a few hours. Then, having wrung out all the gossip we could from each other, one by one we turned to leave, a few going off to bars or to catch flights back home. I was the last one remaining, and as I made to leave, Peter asked, "Have you had dinner?" He began cutting up vegetables for a stew, a process more involved than I had expected. But it was a deliciously sour Garbanese soup, full of bright lemon juice squeezed into vegetable broth.

"This is so good," I said. "I wish the others would've stayed to enjoy this." *aww*

"But you're the only one I wanted to stay." The way he said it, so simply and straightforwardly, like it was the most obvious thing in the world. It was so direct that I couldn't quite look at him, couldn't quite respond. The thing about Peter: He was doglike, by which I mean he inhabited himself without self-consciousness. He didn't second-guess himself or what he wanted. And he liked being petted on the head before sleep, as if I were his owner. Or that was how he made me his owner.

I stayed for a day and a half, before bursting out of his apartment like a swimmer coming up for air.

It was a Tuesday afternoon when I finally left. The Williamsburg Bridge, glimpsed previously from a corner of his alley window, appeared bleached by the unbearably bright sunlight. As I walked over it, looking out across the water, sensing the precipitous drop below as the cables shook with load-bearing trucks, I felt amazed, jostled out of character. I had never done this before. I wasn't the type to stay overnight at a stranger's apartment. I thought, How bizarre that you can be someone else and the world will still absorb you.

This was when Peter lived in New York, before he moved to Chicago to be with me.

The proposal, when it happened, a year after our meeting, was like out of a movie, taking place at a formal restaurant neither of us had been to before. Down on one knee, he resembled so many romantic leads that he could only have been a representation of one. In his palm was a small velvet box. "What's this?" I said, a knot in my stomach. Of course, it was an engagement ring. *A diamond is forever.* I looked at the hard, glittering stone that would outlast us both. I thought, Don't waste your money to accessorize my corpse.

I didn't realize the hardness that had accrued in me.

He was still kneeling, and other diners were watching. I was taking too long. I had always thought I would eventually be married, but it had been an abstract concept, something in the distant future. Yet I was thirty-six already. What if I agreed, on behalf of my future self?

Peter took the ring out of the box. "Try it on. Please."

I extended my hand, and he slipped on the ring. The other diners clapped.

"I bought the ring with award money," Peter said, as we sat down again. It was supposed to be romantic, this trading of creative labor for this symbol of commitment, but I was worried. He saw his writing career as a rocket trajectory, as opposed to the valleys, plateaus, and deserts of most creative careers.

"This must have been very expensive. It's too much." The price of the ring could have sustained a year of writing. I couldn't help myself. "It's just a symbol."

"But it has to be expensive." He looked hurt. "It should cost me something. It signifies the gravity of my commitment."

"Why can't your intention be enough?"

"Because people change. Feelings can be temporary and fickle. That's why it's important to anchor intent to something serious, extravagant."

I looked at the ring. The diamond was surrounded by glittering micro-spawn, mesmerizing at closer glance. "How do you see the future?" I asked.

"Well." He said he believed in traditions, that they have been set in place to guide every generation. He wanted what his parents and grandparents had. He wanted what came before. And that he liked the idea of having heirlooms, material things that would outlast us, that could signify lineage. We had both come from immigrant families. Our parents had taken a great risk and now it was up to us to earn out that risk, build upon what they had established. The immigrant imperative was to buy property and to propagate. "You and me, we're the same," he said. Wasn't it strange that, as a couple, we could communicate only in a second language? I heard the blood in my ears. His voice receded, a faint wavelength from a distant source, until he took my hand, and suddenly the restaurant was too loud and undiscriminating, and our table felt exposed, available to everyone.

"Even if you don't realize it now," he said, referring to the ring, "you'll come to appreciate it in the future. You'll be glad that you have something timeless."

Homecoming begins with an old man, on the cusp of retirement, who learns that the totalitarian regime of his home country has finally been overthrown. Buoyed by a new democratic government, the country has opened its borders to the world. The man had escaped when he was a teen, and had been brought up by a kindly couple in a neighboring country. As an adult, he had worked as a statistical analyst at a life insurance firm and, for most of his adult years, lived a frugal, if unnecessarily ascetic, existence in the same bachelor apartment.

Upon hearing the news, the old man books a ticket to his remote village. There is an excited flurry of preparations. He buys gifts—chocolates, liquor, over-the-counter medications, vitamin supplements, silk scarves, even LEGO sets for imagined nieces and nephews. He has had no contact with his family since his escape, given the restrictiveness of the regime, the remoteness of the village. It is likely that his parents are deceased, but he expects to see his siblings and cousins, and their offspring.

He boards a plane, then a bus, for his return to the village, which is bordered by a winding river. The travel takes a day and a half. The closer he gets, the more familiar the landscape looks, almost identical to how he remembers it. When he walks up the dusty path, still fringed by purple wildflowers, to the old dung home and knocks on the door, his mother opens it. He is speechless with surprise. Then his father steps forward. "Who are you?"

They look exactly as he remembers, but that's exactly the problem.

"I am a traveler," he finally says, giving the most legible version of the truth. He once knew a family in the village, he claims, but hasn't been able to find them.

His parents warmly usher him into the house, where he sees that his siblings are still children. Everyone sits down at the table for dinner, set with the broken utensils he had forgotten about, the defanged forks, the chipped spoons. He touches them with his shaking, liver-spotted hands. His mother places a bowl of stew before him.

"Please eat," she says to the old man. "You have come from so far."

It was late afternoon in the Garboza airport. At the counter with Serk again, in front of the gate I had exited from hours ago, I opened my mouth. Random words poured out of it. "My husband has wandered out of the airport without me. Is there any way I can still enter the country?"

"May I see your passport?" His expression was inscrutable.

My heart sank. "The passports are in the carry-on. He took the carry-on with him when he left."

"Without passport, I cannot let you in Garboza." He said this not so much as a reprimand as a statement of the obvious to a small child. "These are rules."

"I understand. But I do have other documents." I riffled through my tote bag for my wallet, brought out my driver's license. "Here. Does this help?" I knew it probably didn't.

Serk studied the license, glancing back and forth between my face and my picture, taken years ago. He pursed his lips as he assessed whether my past and present selves aligned. "This is you," he confirmed. "But, no good."

"Do you think I can explain to customs that my husband—"

"We are not responsible for . . ." He paused, trying to find the right word. "Marital disputes."

"We weren't having marital disputes," I said. Though that was the problem. We weren't having any disputes at all. I tried again. "My husband, he's not an angry person." Yet I couldn't explain why Peter had stranded me here.

"You don't have phone? Maybe he is at Morning Festival," Serk said, looking out the window.

I followed his gaze. Across the river, the sun was setting over the capital of Garboza. I heard the distant ring of church bells. The festival would begin soon. We didn't have an international phone plan, but even if we had, I was beginning to doubt Peter would pick up. "What would you do if you were in my situation? Should I just . . ." I hesitated. "Should I just reschedule my return flight and leave without him?"

Serk sighed. "Okay, I give you advice. Wait until morning. See what happens."

"Why morning?" I had been in the airport for three hours. An entire night seemed an impossibly long time to wait.

"Because Morning Festival ends in morning. If he comes back, then he returns in the morning."

I looked at him blankly.

"And if he doesn't return," he continued, "then, yes, I book you another flight back to the US. But maybe he returns in the morning." Then, he sharpened his tone. "But you don't have passport, you don't enter Garboza." To reinforce the point, he gestured toward an exit door, manned by a bored security guard, who couldn't have been older than high school age, sitting on a folding chair.

I looked at the guard, then back at Serk. "Is that supposed to scare me?"

Serk smiled, in spite of himself. "Scare or no scare, you wait."

———

When I noticed that the folding chair next to the exit was empty, there was no premeditation. It was an unguarded exit door. I stood up from my seat, walked over, and leaned against the cold push bar. No alarm rang out when it opened, and I slipped outside.

Gooseflesh rippled my arms, reminding me that I had a body, after the hours of listless waiting.

It was dark, except for the bonfire in the distance. The festival was well underway.

I began what would become *Two Weeks* one evening after work, the week I turned twenty-eight. *In the nights leading up to the procedure, she would have this recurring dream of seeing her face entombed behind a layer of cracked ice* was the first line that came to me, seemingly from out of nowhere. *When she checked the dream dictionary in the morning, she learned that cracked ice was a Chinese expression for the pleasures of marriage in old age. This, she decided, was the auspicious sign she had been waiting for, and so did not hesitate in signing the liability waiver.*

From then on, I wrote mostly in the nights after work, at my desk at home, an overheated studio so small it couldn't accommodate a cartwheel. For fresh air, I could reach in front of my desk and force open the window, the tipsy laughter of the neighbors on the stoop suddenly so close. For water, the sink was to the right of the desk. I had the clearest sense of myself then. Everything was within grasping distance. I drank huge amounts of tap water and smoked cigarettes and kept odd hours, staying up as late as I wanted, going to work as tired as I wanted.

I had begun the novel after breaking off an engagement and moving out of my then-boyfriend's apartment. We had been together long enough that the event horizon could only have been marriage. So we had gotten engaged. But the thought of breaking up recurred to me so frequently that it became an inevitability. My ex-fiancé, exasperated that I kept prolonging the wedding planning, finally gave me a talk. "You think marriage is supposed to be a solution to all dissatisfactions of life," he said, "and you're disillusioned because you know marrying me isn't going to solve your other issues. But that's not what marriage is for." *so true → need*

to figure out herself too

This "revelation" didn't prevent us from breaking up, though. I moved out.

In my new studio apartment, I wrote about a married couple, who, during an economic depression, decide to cryogenically freeze themselves to be reanimated in the future, with the understanding that their holdings will significantly appreciate during the time they spend iced: their house, their IRAs, their 401(k)s, their stock portfolio. Given the state of the economy, it was actually cheaper to freeze themselves into the future than to make an earnest effort at a living during this particular period, this political moment.

If I felt stuck in the draft, I would take a walk, bringing along a can of bear Mace the size of a mini fire hydrant, but not very heavy, that my ex-fiancé's father had given me. They were the type of family that camouflaged their wealth in outdoor apparel and camping gear. Whatever equipment my intended in-laws had gifted me, I later sold online to pay the bills. My neighborhood at night, menacing and verdant— fields of bobbing chamomile behind chain-link fences; lurking, dark sedans slowing to a crawl alongside pedestrians; the cheerful blare of music from a fluorescent paleteria—was its own kind of wilderness. I felt thin-skinned, softer, more alert. *more expand + raw*

In the novel, the married couple signs on with a premier cryogenic agency to be frozen for ninety-two years, the maximum amount of time they can afford. Yet, on the morning when they undergo the procedure, the wife's icing chamber suffers a glitch and malfunctions. When the anesthesia wears off, the agency explains to her that she will have to undergo the process again, but given the intense procedural preparations and heavy dose of sedatives, she will have to wait two weeks. She goes home. The majority of *Two Weeks* takes place within the span of those fourteen days, when she is alone and biding her time.

I was twenty-nine, thirty, thirty-one, just biding my time. At some point, I quit my job and lived off my savings, doing occasional freelance work to keep afloat. I kept my overhead low. I stopped going out, and I didn't date. I was always current with rent and bills, but often didn't have enough funds for, say, flights home for Christmas. It's better this way, I thought, to set the precedent that my family shouldn't expect too much from me. I pretended I was free, untethered from their immigrant striving, <u>their expectation that my life should somehow justify their sacrifices.</u> *press uri to accomplish something to make him think it was worth it*

This winter, Y told me that after reading *Two Weeks*, he knew the wife wouldn't go back to the cryogenic agency by the end. She wouldn't submit to being frozen alongside her husband.

"What made you think that?" I asked.

"After the wife is told she has two weeks to kill, she doesn't make any temporary arrangements. She doesn't check into a hotel or stay at a friend's house. Instead, she goes home. She gets her pans out of storage and gets food from her garden. That was the first sign, at least to me, that she wouldn't join her husband."

In the dark, I could see only part of Y's face. We were lying in the upstairs bedroom of his house, where I had spent some time the last few months. In the afternoons before it got dark, I would go over to Y's house to work. He had rolled a desk into the living room, an industrial metal Uline behemoth, where I would spend hours writing, while he worked upstairs in his study. I lost track of time. The night could come on all at once if I wasn't careful.

"I have to get home soon," I told Y. Peter would be returning from teaching his evening class.

"Want me to drive you back?" Y asked this every night. "It's really not an inconvenience."

"I'll just take the bus." The bus ran only during rush hour. If I missed it, I'd just walk.

"This bed doesn't entice you at all?" What Y slept in wasn't even a bed, really; more like a wooden platform with a coverlet laid over it. He did this for the health benefits, claiming that sleeping on hard surfaces was good for a person's back.

I smiled. "I'm too used to my soft bed. I have to get back to my soft life."

"Does your soft life allow for tea before the bus comes?"

"Okay." I got up, and he got up. We went downstairs, descending the staircase where his father had had a cardiac arrest. Y had inherited this house from his dad, who'd lived like a bachelor after his divorce. His mother had kept their old house in the suburbs, and her second husband had moved in. The wall decorations consisted of handmade macramé pieces she had made, a seventies hobby she had revived. Sometimes she would come over, drop off a dish or bags of garden vegetables. I would let her in, and she would place the items in the kitchen without going upstairs to disturb him. She seemed to tolerate me, asking clipped questions and feigning interest in my answers. If she wondered about me and her son, she never asked.

He put the kettle on. In the kitchen, we sipped our tea quietly, leaning against the counter. When I was done, I handed him my mug, and though he wasn't finished drinking his tea, he started washing both our cups in the sink immediately. I cleared away my things from the desk, put them in a backpack.

"Have a good night," I said.

"You too," he replied, not looking at me but at the sink. He was intently scrubbing, swishing the sponge around the rim, where I had left a mark of tinted lip gloss, erasing any trace of my presence. He was still a little afraid of me.

When I think about Y now, I think, He is neither the problem nor the solution.

I walked toward the front door, then looked back. The awkward posture he assumed as he stooped over the low sink, the brittle movements of his arms. All winter long, I had glimpsed his deeply set habits, his regimented schedule. When I left, he would eat a dinner of leftovers, then continue to work until sleep. Everything revolved, to a fault, around work, around his next book project. If I had lived alone, I would have turned out the same way. It is the thing I have been most afraid of happening, my strictness toward myself calcifying into a lifestyle, my traits ingrown so deeply that my oddness surfaces, apparent to all. What I was afraid of in myself, I liked in Y.

I walked outside, leaving him drying the dishes in that rectangle of light, in his kitchen doorway.

In his bedroom, we wouldn't really do anything. After working, we would just lie next to each other, talk by the light of his computer screen saver, which projected a slideshow of extinct animals. The Pyrenean ibex, the Tasmanian tiger, the passenger pigeon, the Mexican grizzly bear, the Baiji white dolphin, found only in the Yangtze River.

"This is the most depressing screen saver," I told him. The computer could've been from the nineties. "They all look like they know they're the last of their kind."

"I'd want to know if I was the last one. Then I could stop the searching for a mate, and just, you know, resign myself." He laughed.

He wasn't very good at sex, the few times we tried. Or maybe I wasn't, having become locked into the conventions of form with the same person for so long. Not to say that Y was bad at it exactly, just peculiar. He was so careful and circumspect, as if I were a weak, delicate handkerchief. He was linear and objective-driven. By analogy, when he finished using a washcloth, he would wring the wet towel in one decisive, calibrated motion so that every drop of water seeped out. In sex, in towel wringing, in dishwashing, as in everything else, he was exactly himself. If being exactly yourself meant you had to suffer the loneliness of being unlike anyone else, he seemed not to mind. The insularity of his lifestyle cradled him. finds being inqui Comforting

It would get pretty cold outside by the evening. People were coming home from the train, lugging their messenger bags and takeout containers, peacefully defeated. What I wouldn't give to escape these late winters in Chicago. Especially the deep, post-holiday extremes of January and February, when, no longer buoyed by festivities and merriments, you're confronted with the empty expanse of a new year, discarded resolutions in your wake, resigned to your own inability to change.

The bus came. I got on, greeted by everyone's haggard faces lit up by the blue screens of their smartphones. The wet floors squeaked beneath my shoes. I stepped over a bag of groceries that had exploded in the aisle, revealing pale palliatives: eggs and yogurt, yogurt and eggs, a broken box of commercial chamomile tea, lemons that rolled around under the seats. It was a whole lifestyle encapsulated in a few items. I picked up a few unbroken eggs, gave them to the woman who was gathering everything back up, a bit humiliated, though it was not her fault.

During the years I lived alone, even in my self-imposed solitude there had been a part of myself I was afraid of. I worked too much, as if it were the only thing, to diminishing returns. Left to my own devices, there was a streak of masochism in my single-minded, obsessive habits. I didn't exercise that much, but when I did, it was in gruesome marathons of overexertion. I didn't eat enough, and when I did, it was in wild, sobering feasts, remembering that I even had a body. I made myself sick. Unregulated, I would have eventually destroyed myself. Yet even knowing this didn't motivate me to change my ways.

I would have continued this lifestyle forever if I hadn't met Peter. Our life was so orderly, grocery shopping on Saturday afternoons and chores on Sundays. I had given in to a natural progression of things. And it was a relief, sort of, to find out that I could live the way everyone else lived, that I was the same as everyone else.

"One day you'll spend the night," Y said.

The night before we left for Garboza, I looked up from the TV to see Peter, standing in the doorway, gazing at me intently. "What's this?" He was holding my spiral-bound notebook. "What is it?" he repeated. He wasn't asking about the whole notebook, we both knew, just the passages that he must have read.

I looked at the page he indicated. "It's fiction," I finally said. It had been a while since we'd read each other's drafts.

I put the movie on mute. On the screen, the countess was prostrating herself before the count, her heaving bosom, stuffed in a ruffled powder blue dress, streaked with tears. It was a confession. She had done something transgressive, and now she was repenting.

He looked from the TV screen to me. "Sorry, I shouldn't have looked," he said, now visibly relaxed. "It's good, if this is your new project. Different, though."

"Different in what way?"

"Well, there's less scene work. It's more emotive. There's more interiority."

"Does it read like a different person wrote it?"

"No, it's still you." He placed the notebook next to me on the sofa, turned back toward the door. "Anyway, I'm going to finish packing."

"It's my journal," I corrected quickly. "It's not fiction."

"It's not fiction?" He stopped in the doorway. Quietly, he said, "I'm assuming these entries are not about me." *anw Ptr*

"They're not about you," I echoed, like an idiot.

"I thought so." His back was toward me, I couldn't see his expression as he put two and two together. "Well, I still have to finish packing," he finally said.

I didn't know what to say either. Numbly, I watched the movie. The duchess was being told that she was forgiven. She burst into tears. Then, out of nowhere, a toddler joined her on-screen, comforting his mother and reestablishing their family. Finally, the count joined his wife and child, kneeling to tearfully embrace them, reestablishing the hegemony of marital unity, of hearth and home. The end credits rolled.

I walked into the other room, where Peter was folding clothes and placing them in our carry-on, and broached the topic carefully. "Maybe I shouldn't go on this trip with you tomorrow."

He didn't look at me. "It's been planned for a while. I think we should follow through."

After a moment, I said, "You can be mad at me. I can take it." *wants him to be mad at*

"You don't have to give me permission to feel my feelings," *hr 4c normal drsrutation* all right?" He finished folding a shirt. "I should feel mad. But the first thought that came to mind was, Is it me?"

I pursed my lips. "I'm not someone who knows what they want. That's the problem."

"Please don't say, It's not you, it's me. That would be tragic." He zipped up the suitcase. "Maybe it's me. Maybe I need to change." He said this last part quietly, as if to himself.

"It's not you, it's—" His glare at my lame attempt at a joke was silencing. I tried again. "Nothing serious happened. You don't have to worry."

He shook his head. "I just feel like this life we have isn't good enough for you. Or I'm not. I'm clearly not . . . what you want. I can't anchor you to this relationship, or to our future."

"What do you mean?"

He looked at me. "Did you look at those house listings our agent sent us?"

"No, not yet." I knew what was coming.

"Well, that's what I mean." He sighed, but tried not to show it. "I feel like I'm the only person working for our future, like taking on those extra classes to save for the down payment. Meanwhile, you can't even be bothered to line up some house viewings."

"I know." I couldn't do better than to say that.

"The thing is," he continued, "I think you do want the same things that I want. It's just that you don't know what you want until you're confronted with it. You want it only when you have it."

"We need to talk about this more. It's a longer discussion." I circled back to the topic of the trip. "But tomorrow, I shouldn't go to Garboza with you."

"No, I want you to come." Of this, he seemed the most certain. "They call it the Morning Festival because everything looks new in the morning. So I think, at least symbolically, it'll be good for us to witness this festival together."

"Are you sure?"

He didn't seem to hear me, having returned to his packing. "You know, the future sneaks up on you before you know it."

On the plane, before liftoff, I took an Ambien. He didn't need to change. I needed to change. I didn't wake up until we had landed.

The town of Garboza was only a mile or so from the airport. You could see the bonfire, where people gathered, in the distance. The air grew smokier on the route toward the town. Once you found the road on the other side of the river, it led you where you needed to go, weaving through a wooded area before passing stone houses, a gas station, the occasional storefront as you neared. They sat darkened and snuffed out, as if before the invention of electricity.

It was part of the ritual, the town turning off all its lights for one night. In order for the miraculous to take place, Peter had explained, the town had to make a gesture of collective sacrifice.

As I came closer, the light from the bonfire seemed abnormally bright.

The bonfire pit was situated in an old, large concrete fountain. As I approached, I was surprised by the scattered attendance, a few dozen townsfolk outfitted in funeral clothes, lazing around the fire. Two men played a game that looked like Go as a handful of people watched, and a few women drank wine and talked among themselves, while their children slept on the grass beside them. Some adults also seemed to be napping. Instead of a celebratory, festive mood, the proceedings had a lethargic air. Everyone seemed to be waiting.

There was a violinist playing mournful solos while standing on a wooden crate. The melody was similar to something Peter used to sing in the shower.

I scanned the figures. I walked around the fire, considering each person carefully, trying to identify him. A woman, lifting her mourning veil to put a cigarette to her lips, scrutinized me as she smoked. I wasn't dressed for the occasion. My black clothes for the festival had been in the shared suitcase Peter had taken.

When one song ended, another began. It was also familiar.

I didn't see him.

Presently, a priest walked around the diminishing fire, dipping a ladle into a bucket of holy water and dousing it. He did this slowly, meticulously. His aim, it appeared, was not to immediately extinguish the fire, but to temper it. I assumed that all the participants had already thrown their resolutions into the fire earlier in the festivities.

"Excuse me," I said to the priest. He was a small, dark man with light eyes. "I'm looking for my husband. Have you seen him?" And I took out my wallet and showed him a picture. "Petru."

He gestured for me to bring the picture closer. "Ah! I know Petru. Ever since he was a boy, he would come back every summer. When someone leaves Garboza, they don't come back very often. But Petru, he comes back almost every summer. He is very loyal. This is unusual." He passed the picture back to me, then paused. "You are his wife?"

"Yes. It's my first time in Garboza."

He nodded. "Ah. You should have come years ago. People from all over the world would fly to the Morning Festival. Lots of tourists, visitors from around the world. It was much more busy back then." He sighed. "We still continue our traditions. This is more for townspeople now."

"Well, maybe it's better to have a more homey, intimate

festival . . ." I trailed off, then asked the question I wanted to ask. "Do you know where Petru is?"

"Everyone who is transforming, they are in the forest." He pointed toward the woods, some meters away. There was a path leading into it.

"What are they doing there?"

"They are transforming. We put them in the dirt, in the earth. We will see what they look like in the morning."

"Can I . . . can I go and find Petru?" I gestured to the forest.

The priest tsked, the first sign of irritation. "No, no. You're too late. It's already begun." He cleared his throat. "The transformations happen in the dark. It's very delicate. When you observe someone's process against their will, you interrupt it. They need to be alone."

"Are they really buried in the ground?" I thought back to what Amina had said.

He smiled. "The soil of the forest, Garboza Forest, is very old, and it is very rich." He raised his finger to his lips, then gestured for me to listen.

I listened. It was a faint sound, a kind of humming that, on careful listening, distinguished itself as a low moaning. "It sounds like animals."

"Humans are animals too, are they not? When an animal is sick, it goes alone by itself to find a quiet place in the woods and rests, for days, for weeks. Sometimes it cannot overcome its illness, but many times it can. The resting, the quiet, and being alone is enough. This is the way of nature. Nature corrects itself." The priest seemed almost to be talking to himself now. Then he cleared his throat. "Anyway, you wait. You wait until morning. They come out of the forest, and you can see how they've changed. You will know Petru when you see him. You will recognize him."

Then he resumed his ladling of the water onto the fire, which hissed in protest.

At the end of *Two Weeks*, the wife lives the rest of her life alone in the house she once shared with her husband, while he remains in cryogenic sleep. Though she never remarries, she gives birth to a daughter, who begets another daughter. Before her passing, the wife instructs the granddaughter to meet her frozen husband when he has awoken. "Take care of him, please." Upon waking, the dazed husband initially mistakes the granddaughter for his wife.

In the years that follow, the granddaughter visits him regularly at the house he once shared with his wife, bringing him meals and doing some caretaking around the garden, which has overtaken the backyard. She snips the vegetables that are ready to be harvested, plants flowers that she later cuts and displays in the home. He is not an old man by any means, but he acts like one, dazed and out of sorts with a world he doesn't recognize. Though he is now independently wealthy (his carefully curated stock portfolio paid out), he drifts from day to day without much in the way of plans.

One afternoon in the garden, he reaches out to touch her hand. But she bats it away without a thought. "I'm not your wife, old man," the granddaughter of his wife says with a laugh. Then she dusts off her apron and heads back home, where she lives alone.

There had been a snowstorm. I had stayed the night. What had looked like an afternoon flurry had steadily intensified, so that by evening, all public transit was suspended. Though Y offered to drive me back, he couldn't even get his car out of the driveway. "The easiest thing would be if you stayed over," he said. I agreed, and called Peter, who had just arrived home, to let him know.

We had lived in this city long enough to know that before a snowstorm, it's best to stock up on provisions. So we walked across the street to the market, which I realized, trailing behind Y under fluorescent lights, was an Eastern European grocery. Being a creature of habit, Y moved through the aisles on autopilot, picking up sacks of onions and rice. But I was dazzled by the novelty of other products—Croatian sour cherry juice, Bulgarian sheep yogurt, Ukrainian sunflower halvah, Russian black bread, Greek mountain tea and chamomile flowers, Iranian cardamom sugar cubes. Plus logs of

Amish butter, containers of microgreens, and homemade dill pickles. Whatever I pointed out, he placed in the cart. Though I wouldn't be around long enough to enjoy them.

For dinner, he made a kind of rutabaga soup, with dill and celery seed. It was his mother's recipe. She would make it one of two ways, a "weekday" or a "weekend" version. "For you, we will make it weekend-style," he said, adding a scoop of sheep's yogurt for a richer broth.

I toasted big slabs of black bread and made a seltzer drink with the sour cherry juice.

We ate the soup in his kitchen, sitting at barstools behind the counter, illuminated by the awkward overhead lighting. Through the kitchen window above the counter, I could see the sheets of snow coming down, being blown in different directions. Coinciding with the shrill screech of the wind, the walls of the house shook. There was no question the house would hold.

Because I felt happy, because the happiness was a tenuous sensation that might have dissipated if I'd breathed differently, I didn't broach the subject until after dinner. At which point I told Y, ripping the Band-Aid off quickly, "In another few days, I'm leaving for a trip to Garboza with Peter. I'll be gone for about a week." There was a pause while I took a breath. Then: "But I won't be coming back here after that."

There was a moment before Y spoke. "Why are you going?" he asked.

"The trip is kind of a belated honeymoon. We've planned

it for a long time." Left unspoken was the idea that the trip was supposed to reset our marriage.

"I don't think you want this." He was saying this carefully. He was looking down at the seltzer. "I don't think this is you."

It was true, I didn't particularly want to go to Garboza at this point. "Maybe it's not what I want now," I conceded, "but it's something I will want in the future. If I don't go, I'll regret not having made more of an effort in my marriage."

"If something is not what you want now, then how do you know it's something you'll want in the future?"

"My situation is different from yours," I finally said. "You can do whatever you want."

"You seem to do what you want." There was a coolness in his voice, and we both dropped the matter at hand.

After dinner, he made a bed for me by sheeting his sofa in the living room. Y retreated upstairs, and I lay down, more tired than I'd realized. I looked up at the ceiling while snow continued blitzing outside the living room windows. The shadows of the snowfall against the streetlights put me to sleep.

When I think about Y now, I think less about the beginning than about the end, which is where all my feelings have now pooled, having rolled downward toward the inevitable outcome.

After I left his house, after I stopped seeing him, I would

give myself over to magical thinking, conjuring up solutions that might magically summon Y to me. Poetry didn't bring him to me. The poems I read listlessly were only beacons reflecting my feelings. They were sirens that wept the same way I wept. Plus, Y didn't read poetry. Given that he didn't vibrate on similar poetic frequencies, even the most lyrical lines couldn't be used as incantations to conjure him psychically. Astrology didn't bring him to me. Our signs were not compatible. According to online sources, water negates fire. Or something like that. Even though my moon was in his sign, dragging his tides, there was simply not enough astrological synchronicity. My body didn't bring him back to me. I had already offered the mealy cornucopia of my body and it didn't do anything. I think what he liked was a certain type of innocence. Not someone young or naïve exactly, but someone who was more straightforward and open, with legible intentions. And possessing the quality of sweetness. (I have sweetness too, just underneath thicker rinds.) He didn't like neurotic women, women who were unclear, who acted out their anxieties, who said one thing and meant another.

I slept fitfully through the night. Periodically, the house shook with a gust of wind. The steam radiators hissed. I would open my eyes to a dark and cavernous room. And maybe it was just a dream, but at some point I thought I saw Y's face, looking at mine. He wanted to say something.

I might've been dreaming. If it had been him, if he was going to say more to me, I didn't want to hear it. He is neither the problem nor the solution.

In the morning, I woke up early, even before the roads had been cleared. I folded up the blankets and got dressed. The fir branches had become frozen to the door, but they yielded with a good yank.

I woke up alone, in front of a pile of cinders that had once been the bonfire. There was no one else around. Instinctively, I knew to go to the forest, to the opening that the priest had forbidden me from walking through the night before. I didn't have to venture far inside the wooded area to see where others had gathered. I did not see Peter. And it wasn't until I came closer that I noticed the covered plots in the ground. I had trampled across a few, winding my way toward the crowd.

They were clustered around the priest and the violinist, who were digging up one of the plots. It was a shallow hole, not six feet deep, like a proper grave would be. Then again, based on Peter's tales of Garboza, they didn't bury their dead that deep here.

Out of the earth emerged an old, dusty man, who dazedly took the hands of the priest as he climbed out. A few people, who I suspected were family, came up to him. They seemed to inspect his neck and shoulders, and they said something in

Garbanese to the crowd. A smattering of applause. The man bowed toward everyone, suddenly prideful. Then he turned around, showing his body. Whatever was supposed to heal had healed.

The priest and the violinist moved on to the next plot.

From this one emerged a middle-aged woman, shivering but smiling. Her husband and child came to receive her. She lifted her arm, it seemed, for their inspection. The child exclaimed excitedly. Then the husband drew his wife's arm up, as if she were a boxing champ, and addressed the crowd. Again, we all clapped. Again, we moved on.

The informality of the proceedings, the lack of ceremony, surprised me. A baby was crying, exacerbating my morning headache. Out of anxiety, I scanned the crowd again for Peter. I knew, though, that he was buried in one of those plots somewhere. Would I even be able to recognize him when he emerged? What could he have possibly changed?

The third plot yielded a child of about eight, whose mother rushed forward to claim him. He spun around and around in front of his mother, who kept pinching his right arm and marveling at whatever change had taken place. She thwacked her son on the back, shaking loose the clods of dirt that covered him, and then, with the most casual nonchalance, they walked out of the forest together in the middle of the applause, leaving the group of us behind.

We went to the fourth and the fifth graves, the sixth and the seventh. By the way each of those uncovered displayed their body to the crowd, and the way we all clapped, it seemed that most participants had been healed of some physical ailment. I deduced that one person had emerged with a straightened spine.

The plots were scattered across the forest floor in a haphazard, unplanned fashion. The participants had all dug their holes themselves, and without collective planning. Though the priest cleared the plots within the immediate vicinity, others were more difficult to find, behind large stones or fallen trees. The crowd often pointed them out.

At the eighth plot, the buried person did not rouse, did not emerge from the ground. The priest stooped down, checked the uncovered body's pulse. Then he said the person's name, and the family flocked around. The priest said a few words to the family, which I couldn't hear.

He continued on to the next plot.

I was holding my breath. What had happened? The baby's crying was soon subsumed by another sound: the wailing of the family surrounding the eighth plot. They dragged him out of the earth, holding him, this man, this father and patriarch. They bore him to their chests, beating his back as if to beat the life back into him.

The rest of the crowd looked on, stony-faced, including the priest. But they kept moving. If anything, the family's sorrow seemed to give more momentum to the procedure, to the urgency of the situation.

We finished the ninth, the tenth, the eleventh plots, the family's cries of mourning growing fainter and fainter as we moved away. The Morning Festival did not allow for grief, it seemed. If the transformation didn't work, it didn't work.

After the fifteenth plot or so, I noticed another one close to the riverbank. It seemed like an impractical place to bury oneself, underneath all that damp soil. Next to the plot was a suitcase, lying askew on its side. It was our carry-on. I can't say why I felt the instinct to hide. I stepped behind a tree and watched as the priest and the violinist came to Peter's plot. Before they began digging, the priest looked around at the thinning crowd, trying to locate me, maybe. Then he turned to the task at hand, taking the shovel to the dirt.

I watched as they began to dig, wincing when I felt they drove the spade too deep into the earth, worried that they might accidentally hit skin. Though they worked at the same pace as before, it seemed to me that they were digging for far longer than at the other sites. The violinist stopped to wipe his brow.

Again, the priest looked around at the thinning crowd.

And then, I couldn't help myself. I came out from behind the tree and ran up to the plot, scooping handfuls of earth. The priest touched my shoulder, but I didn't stop. I just wanted to uncover his head at least, I just wanted to see his face. The crowd murmured uneasily, the emotive American. I dug until I touched skin, and a patch of flesh became visible. There was his nose, then his cheeks. I cleared soil from the hollows of his eyes. They remained closed, but emitted a wetness, like tears.

The priest touched my shoulder again. "Stop, please. Let us do this."

Peter opened his eyes. In that moment, his face was very still. It was the same face, but blank.

I said his name once, then twice, until finally, his eyes focused on me. They were the same eyes. He blinked a few times, trying to see. There was no indication, at least not yet, that he recognized me. Rather, he appeared stunned, new to himself. And so he was new to me too, in that moment of uncertainty. I was trying to see what had changed, how he had changed. Maybe the transformation was invisible. There was nothing I could immediately identify. "Peter," I said again. Then: "Petru. Petru."

We looked at each other.

So maybe a good transformation; a fresh start

Office Hours

How she used to smoke in his office, back when the University allowed that in campus buildings. He didn't smoke, but allowed her to as she sat on the sofa across from his desk. Or rather, he didn't object, and even set out a little dessert plate as an ashtray. Maybe because it gave them both a pretense for talking longer, for the extra duration of a cigarette, then two, then three. So that by the time she graduated, she was a chain-smoker.

She had taken several of his courses, mostly on cinema. She read the assigned Gombrich texts, studied the Muybridge prints, wrote a paper on close-ups of Falconetti's face. After class, she would drop by his office hours to continue their class discussion. "Let's hear it" was the first thing he'd say when she arrived. During her junior year, they would talk for an hour every week.

Over time, their conversations began to drag, usually when he started pontificating about how he'd never intended to be a career academic, and devolved into complaints about the institution. Though flattered that he confided in her, she grew a little bored. He had the dream job of watching movies and writing about them.

He was both an involved mentor who frequently solicited her opinions and a raging, pacing animal, sour about where he had ended up in life.

Once, she had offhandedly mentioned that she was tired and couldn't wait to sleep. "So go home then," he snapped. Taken aback, she explained that she didn't have enough time to go home before her next class. "You can take a nap," he said, and offered to leave his office so she could sleep on the sofa.

"Where would you go?" she asked.

"I'll go to Holy Grounds," he said, referring to the basement coffee shop in Godspeed Hall. He shuffled some papers on his desk. "I'll take these papers to grade with me."

Except when she lay down, he didn't leave. Maybe she'd already known he wouldn't. He had remained behind his desk, and the sound of pages turning, the quick swipes of the pen as he scrawled devastating comments on students' papers, served as the white noise that lulled her to sleep. She thought of his pen scrawling over her body, his sharp razor-point tip marking her with corrective feedback in corrosive industrial ink.

When she awoke, he already had his coat on. "Okay?" he had asked as she sat up.

"Okay," she said, a little embarrassed. "Was I asleep for long?"

"No, not at all," he said. "But office hours end in two minutes."

Whereas she had wanted to be the object of his gaze a little longer. She liked being warmed by his interest without ever yielding to it. The naps began to occur, if not frequently, then enough to set a precedent. The rust-colored sofa was mushy but comfortable. He never seemed to mind, and after a while, she no longer felt self-conscious about languishing in the amnion of his office. When she woke up, he would say, "Okay?" and she would reply, "Okay," and leave.

It was a drafty office. She seemed to hear wind whistling from the walls. Leaving Godspeed Hall, she would bury her face in the collar of her coat, redolent of a tangy pine, not of him exactly, but of his office, as she walked across campus on those winter afternoons, the sky already dark.

There was no sofa in her apartment, no bed. She slept on an inflatable mattress, reinforced nightly with a bike pump. Her parents had remortgaged their house to afford her private-college tuition, and she didn't ask for more. With her wages shelving books at the library, she subsisted on spaghetti and apples. These were supplemented by appetizer spreads laid out at receptions following English Department events. After lectures on the decline of the novel, the failures of empire, she pilfered smoked salmon, soft cheeses, even the decorative garnishes—starfruit slices, caviar ruffles.

On weekends, there was usually a party. Her classmates, freed from their wealthy families, cosplayed as struggling intellectuals. With ham-handed irony, they put out cellophane-wrapped Twinkies, Ding Dongs, MoonPies on faux-silver trays, snacks they wouldn't eat themselves. Their privilege was always betrayed by some outlandish gesture, like a mariachi band, in full regalia, hired to play in the living room. If the potent coke, the immaculate sound system didn't tip you off. The careless way they walked through snow in suede Nikes.

The last time she remembered seeing the Professor was after leaving one such party, a few weeks before graduation. She had been standing on a street corner late at night, waiting for a ride. It had begun to rain lightly. He had been walking his dog. Like most older faculty, he lived near campus.

"I like your dog, Professor," she had called out. It was an excessive, girthful dog, a slobbering Bernese mix.

"Oh, good," he said, as he neared. "My dog is your dog."

"Oh, good. I was about to clone it. What's its name?"

"Nemo."

"Hi, Nemo! Nemo, did you know that your name means 'no one'? I'm sorry!" The dog withstood her overzealous petting with sober dignity.

The Professor also waited until she was done. "Do you have a strategy for getting home?"

"Yes." She didn't mention that she had been waiting for "the drunk van," a campus weekend service that deposited inebriated students at home.

He studied her, then pointed across the street, at God-speed Hall. "That's my office."

"I know." Though actually she hadn't known. Her surroundings suddenly reoriented themselves around her: she had been standing on the wrong corner for pickup. "It's a nice office."

"Thank you. If you'd like to dry off, you're welcome to it." He added, clarifying, "I could give you the keys. I won't be in until Monday."

"I'm fine." She smiled to show him so.

"I see." He hesitated. "You're graduating in two weeks. What's next after this?"

"I don't have anything lined up." On the other side of graduation was her actual life, the slow narrowing of possibilities that would catch her and freeze her in a vocation, a relationship, a life. She intended to avoid that slow calcification for as long as possible—if only by refraining from making any crucial choices. In other words, she was moving back home. She added, "I want your job one day." Maybe she was saying it just to see his response.

He smiled. "You can have it. This is my last year."

"You're retiring?" The surprise of this news sobered her a little.

"I've probably overstayed. Once you're tenured, you never leave." Nemo tugged on his leash, but the Professor made no indication to move. "Meanwhile, the gap between you and your students widens. You get older, while they stay the same age, year after year. Like vampires."

"Well, sounds pretty nice to me, at least the tenure part." She didn't know what to say. He was not happy. He was just a person. "I've really enjoyed your classes, Professor." She wanted to add more. How watching long films in the campus screening room, as they did in his class, made the Midwestern winters bearable; how she appreciated his clear, straightforward lecture style; and how, unlike other faculty, he never wielded his knowledge as a weapon against his students. She lacked the finesse in the moment to convey this.

He was still speaking, had been for a while, trying to give last words, advice. "The sanest way forward—you have to learn how to split yourself up, like an earthworm."

She didn't know what he was talking about. Instead, she followed his gaze to Godspeed Hall, then looked back and forth between them. It made her dizzy. "Whoa," she said aloud, to herself.

"I think Nemo is getting restless. I should be on my way." He nodded at her. "Get home safe. And if I don't see you before graduation, stay out of trouble."

Stay out of trouble. There it was. She didn't like how he code-switched at his whim, <u>wavering between treating her like a peer and like just another student</u>. As if he had never encouraged those hour-long discussions in his office, or called her a <u>kindred spirit</u>. Maybe he was demonstrating that he could dictate the terms of their association however he chose. *→ makes it confusing for her then*

She watched as the Professor walked across the street with Nemo. They ambled across the quad, then entered Godspeed Hall, where, through the stairwell windows, she saw him enter the third floor, where his office was located. The clocktower indicated that it was nearing three in the morning.

She did not know him that well, she reminded herself. She had just been his student, a vampire. Whatever he was doing, it was really none of her business.

Her default position was that of a dog fighting out of a corner. For much of her adult life, she had assumed this defensive crouch, tensed to prove herself against all odds at all times. She did not have the assurance, like many of her peers, that if one thing didn't work out, there would always be something else. Maybe this desperation was how she had managed to end up on the tenure track, doggedly persisting through a complicated gauntlet of grad school and postdocs and fellowships until she finally found herself gainfully employed

likes the security tenured work gives her

as an assistant professor at her college alma mater, where the fights were imperceptible because everyone had too much to lose, and there was no corner.

followed what he wanted to himself

The Film and Media Studies faculty holiday party was held in a circular brick tower that typically served as the department conference room. She sipped rosé next to the window, a heavy wool coat over her other arm as if she were ready to leave. Surveying the event space, she did the usual reconnaissance: There was the one who bludgeoned her with compliments, vague in content, exclamatory in delivery. There was the one who always cut her off midsentence. There was the one who leaned in too closely and asked, in a hushed, solemn voice, "So how are you doing?," as if only they could be the facilitator of her feelings. This dance of feigned, unearned intimacies, playing on endlessly at every meeting.

not built on anything real

But anyway. She was showing her face. She was engaging. And Carolyn was half-heartedly feting her.

"Hey, before I forget. To your book," Carolyn said, raising her glass and clinking it against hers. "Will you sign my copy?"

"Absolutely," Marie replied, though no copy materialized.

"You must be so busy after book release. I'm sure you're being heaped with accolades."

face+face

"I'm just glad it's done." Her book, on cinema of "the face," had been released by a university press at the beginning of the semester.

Studying face like she did in his class

Carolyn leaned in meaningfully. "How are you feeling about that?"

Marie wasn't entirely sure what the question was. "Well, it always takes longer than you think." She cleared her throat. "Do you have any interesting plans for holiday break?"

"We're taking the kids to the Adirondacks. We all need the detox, you know?" Carolyn waved her jittery hands, glistening with rings. "It's crazy how busy things get during the semester. I'm serving on, like, ten committees." She looked at Marie curiously.

"Ladies." Sean approached, placing his hands on both their backs. He was her least favorite. "I presume you're teaching next semester."

"Yes." Carolyn and Marie nodded in unison.

"I presume these courses have titles." Sean looked at Marie. He didn't ask her questions so much as issue statements that she could either confirm or refute.

"Well, one course is called The Disappearing Woman," Marie said. "We start with the genre of women's films, then we look at contemporary heroines. You know, *Vertigo*, *L'avventura* . . ."

He sipped his wine, glanced around the room. "Oh, that's fun," he said, after waving at the program chair across the room. She couldn't tell if he was pretending, this nonchalance. "So I assume the woman always disappears by the end."

"I guess the course title should come with a spoiler alert." She too sipped her drink.

"You know, I've found in my experience that students respond best to genre surveys rather than courses built around a theme." So passive aggressive bro

"Depends on the syllabus, I'm sure," she said benignly. He hadn't been teaching at the University much longer than she had, maybe a year or two. She turned to Carolyn. "What are you teaching this spring, Carolyn?"

"Oh, just an introductory survey to silent film." Carolyn shifted warily. "I have to run. I promised the sitter I wouldn't be late tonight." shut up !

"Anyway," Sean resumed, ignoring Carolyn's retreat. "I would take a look at some of the course listings from years past to give you the right idea of what works best."

"I have, but thanks." Marie looked around the room, scanning it for reasons to excuse herself. Colleagues encircled one another, then broke apart periodically to form new groups.

She spotted the Professor, speaking to someone across the room. She startled. It wasn't his appearance that was surprising—though he looked, for lack of more elegant descriptors, frail and decrepit. She hadn't seen him in maybe fifteen years, not since college. She'd thought he had moved away after retirement.

On cue, he looked up and caught her gaze.

The Professor wanted to see his old office, which now happened to be her office. And so they walked across the dimly

funkiness again

lit quads in the snow. He walked with a cane, and hid his winces with every step. He was speaking to her as if they were picking up mid-conversation, across the span of more than a decade. He said, "I'm very ill. The treatments aren't working."

"Is it serious?" she asked, knowing well that at his age, all illnesses were serious.

"It's terminal," he said matter-of-factly. "I don't have long, though there are differing opinions about how long."

"I'm sorry." Her pat response sounded so trivial. They made their way to Godspeed Hall in silence.

When she opened the door to her office and switched on the fluorescent lights, he looked around at the now-bare walls and new, plywood furnishings, the empty bookcases, the little mini-fridge plugged into the corner outlet. She wanted to apologize for not having properly made the space her own.

He turned to her. "You don't use this office?"

She thought of how she used to nap on his rust-colored sofa, now gone. "It's mostly just for meeting with students." She preferred to do her scholarly work at home. "Anyway, would you like some tea?" When he didn't respond, she said, "Is there any drink that you would like?"

"I would like you to keep an open mind." He was studying the closet behind the desk. Then he opened the door, revealing an old armoire, the only piece of furniture that remained from his time. She watched as he struggled to move it.

"Here, let me help you," she said. But he had already slid

it to the edge of the closet. From the drag marks in the floorboards, it had probably been moved this way many times.

"There," he said, satisfied. "Now turn on the light, please."

When she pulled the drawstring, the bare bulb dangling from the ceiling clicked on. The light revealed a hole in the wall, something that she had never noticed before. It was large enough that a person could easily enter it.

"Is this extra storage space?" She knew it was not.

"No, but you'll see." He stepped through the hole until he was almost fully submerged inside the wall. She didn't move. Sensing her hesitation, he turned around. "Okay?"

"Okay." As if in a dream, she followed him.

On the other side is where the story begins.

The passageway led outside. She looked around, allowing her eyes to adjust to the darkness. To their left, a cloister of coniferous trees, swaying in the breeze. It had stopped snowing. Or, actually, there was no snow on the ground at all. It was not even cold. The air felt soft and supple. It was almost warm, a summer's night.

She said, "I have never been to this part of campus before." And then waited for him to correct her. They were not on campus, or even near it.

"I used to come out here when I had your office." He was still looking around.

There was a full moon in the sky, the only source of light. It illuminated what looked like a country road, a two-lane stretch that receded into the distance.

She wanted to take off her coat, but to do so would have been to accept the plausibility of her surroundings. "Where are we, Professor?"

He pointed to a pine tree some yards away. "Do you see that cup over there? On the ground?" She squinted. There was a white paper cup at its base. "It's a cup of coffee. Can you take a look?"

She walked over to the tree and picked it up. It was a Solo cup, filled with what appeared to be fresh coffee, lightened with cream. "It's a cup of coffee," she echoed.

"Is it still warm?"

"Yes." She brought it to him, but he didn't bother to examine it.

"What if I told you I left it there years ago, on my last day before retirement?"

"But it's still warm." Heat emanated from the cup.

"Yes, that's my point." He paused. "What I can tell you is that I have visited this place hundreds of times, at all hours, across all seasons. It is always night here. The weather is always the same, warm and temperate."

She studied the coffee cup in her hand. The paper sleeve was imprinted with the logo of Holy Grounds, which had closed years ago.

She looked around again, studied the space. "Where does that road go?" she asked, gesturing to the two-lane freeway.

"I don't know. I've never seen a single car go down it." He was looking at the sky, the full moon. "It's always the same," he reiterated.

She set the cup down in the grass. It had been burning her hand. "Why did you show this to me?" she asked. When he didn't answer, she repeated the question.

It was only after the Professor had passed, during holiday break, that she entered the passageway again. The University memorial service, scheduled shortly after New Year's, was held in the same circular tower room as the faculty holiday party.

She had not expected the body to be on view, half the casket opened to expose his face, pale and frowning. Looking at this presentation, she felt that she didn't understand anything.

Something he had once said in a lecture: "It is in the most surreal situations that a person feels the most present, the closest to reality." What film had he been speaking of? She wished she could ask him now.

Sean approached, clearing his throat. "So I hear you're presenting at HFF."

"I think I'm subbing for someone else who wasn't available," she obliged. She moved away from the coffin, not wanting to hold the conversation so close to the body. Sean followed.

"Huh, so you replaced someone." He took a sip of wine.

"That's my impression. But I don't know." She was downplaying it. The Humanities Futures Forum—or "huff," as everyone called HFF—was an annual weekend fundraising event, attended by major donors to the University. Though everyone bemoaned it as a dog and pony show, that didn't prevent the scorekeeping over who was asked to present.

He was looking at her, not saying anything.

After a pause, she asked, "What about you? Are you presenting at HFF?"

He ignored her question. "I presume you have ideas about what you're presenting."

What if she just didn't respond? "I'm not sure yet. Maybe something on cinematic fantasy or dream spaces. Like *Wizard of Oz*, or maybe *Stalker*."

"Fantasy space." He nodded slowly. "Well, you could devote the entire session to all the Tarkovsky films alone."

"It's just a twenty-minute presentation." She held her smile. "But I'll keep that in mind."

"But, c'mon, Tarkovsky. There are so many films that would fit that theme. It would be easy to create a presentation just around that." He looked at her closely, waiting for her to acquiesce. "Wouldn't it?"

Marie smiled benignly. "I should go and pay my respects."

In her time at the University, she had begun to dislike Sean intensely, but as a point of pride she couldn't quite commit to her dislike. He seemed unworthy of any intensity of feeling, he who made his students call him Doctor.

But today, at the beginning of the new year, at the memorial for her former professor, the prospect of seeing someone like Sean regularly, of forever dodging him at receptions and cocktail parties, of treading lightly while serving on the same committees, of presenting at faculty meetings, just seemed intolerable, fucking impossible.

During holiday break, she had been thinking of leaving the University. Then she thought of leaving academia altogether. When she brainstormed about what else she would do, where else she would go, her mind drew a blank.

Across the room, attendees clustered around the Professor's widow, elegant in her charcoal dress, and their surviving grown children, who had flown in from East Coast cities. "He wanted to go on his own terms," the widow said. "He decided when he wanted to stop the treatment. So I'm glad he was able to wield some control over the process, at least."

"And what about you? How are you doing?" Carolyn cooed to the bereaved woman. "I am so sorry. You must be so exhausted. Now, please tell me there's someone taking care of you." Her voice was subsumed by the cicada chorus of others' condolences, their voices metallic and mercenary.

Marie placed her glass on a table and left.

It was still bright outside, at least for a January afternoon. She walked across the quads, and retreated to her office, where tears did not come. In the silence of not crying, she heard the wind whistling from the closet. Of course she moved the armoire. Of course she stared at the opening. Hostile to new knowledge, she had not been into the passageway since he had first shown it to her.

Now she entered again, for the first time by herself.

When she emerged on the other side, it was night, just as it had been before. The towering pine trees rustled in greeting, unloosening a familiar pine scent. The inky sky above hosted a scattering of stars, the full moon.

She moved through the clearing uneasily, aware of the exit at all times.

Spotting something on the ground, she saw it was the paper cup of coffee, where she had placed it last. It was still warm. Hot, even. She took a sip, scalding her tongue. Then she downed the rest of the cup.

On Wednesdays, she taught The Disappearing Woman. The class consisted of a screening followed by a discussion. That week, in the February thaw of spring semester, they watched *Ghost World*, released in 2001, a year many of her students had been born. In the end, Enid, the teenage protagonist, gets on a mysterious bus and seems to leave town. The credits rolled.

Marie flipped on the fluorescent lights in the screening room, and looked around at the fifteen students. "So, what did you think?" She liked to begin with general questions, allowing the students to choose the topics, before she zoomed in on specific subjects.

After a moment, Zach spoke. "I didn't get the ending. I mean, I like that it's kind of open-ended, but it feels like a cop-out. Enid just gets on this special bus and goes where?"

She tried to reset the question, to anchor them in the source material. "Well, the ending seems to serve as a refutation of some kind, with Enid opting out of the town on this mysterious bus. One way to approach this is to ask: What is *Ghost World* trying to refute? Are there specific scenes that suggest an answer?"

When Marie started out as a teacher, she had directed all her efforts toward appearing unafraid. But training yourself not to appear afraid was not the same as training yourself not to *feel* afraid, the difference between pretending and being. She had taught long enough that as soon as she slipped into the classroom, she became another person entirely.

"There's a lot of anxiety around this idea of authenticity," Abby offered. "Like, the fake-fifties diner that plays Top 40 music. Or the art teacher who has these narrow parameters for what qualifies as art. Enid and Rebecca are always hyperaware of what's inauthentic."

"Yeah, but wherever Enid ends up, she's only going to see inauthenticity and hypocrisy. There is no place she's going where she's *not* going to see that," said Grey. "What kind of place could the bus take her that would meet her standards? That place doesn't exist."

Sarah added, "Enid gets to disappear, but most of us can't do that. Most of us are like Rebecca: we're critical of the world but we still have to live in it."

Abby interjected: "But that's the fantasy, right? That there is an escape, there is a way out of . . ." She trailed off, then restarted. "The movie doesn't show you the answers. The ending simply opts out. It's an aversion."

After class, Marie returned to her office and, through the closet, entered the passageway. She referred to the outside area as "the chamber." Initially, it had served as a discreet area to smoke, a habit she had picked up again after the Professor's memorial. It was often after class that she did this, or before a long faculty meeting, or in the middle of a lecture by a visiting scholar. She would lock her office door, remove the armoire, and go through the wall. She lingered in the clearing near the entryway, blowing her smoke into the cool night air, surrounded by those swaying trees. The pleasure of this place was its extreme, surreal privacy.

Over time, her visits had become more exploratory.

In the chamber, there was the road and there were the

woods. She skirmished in the woods occasionally, but didn't venture far. There was the sound of water, a brook, maybe, but she never went in that direction. The Professor had said he didn't know how large the forest was. He had gotten lost there once, and had emerged days later, at a loss to explain his disappearance to his wife, who had filed a missing person report. He had warned Marie not to get lost.

Using a key chain flashlight to guide her, Marie walked along the silent road, which hosted no vehicles, no cars. She would never get lost if she stuck close to it; it would always lead her back to the entryway. There were flowers that grew in the ditches, thistle and yarrow and hyssop, some sagebrush and chamomile. She went for a mile this way in the moonlight, collecting flowers in her hands. She didn't know how far the road unfurled, but she had never reached its end. The deeper she went inside the chamber, the more apprehension she felt. She would only walk for as far as she could walk back.

The road reminded her of her lost year. After graduation, she had moved back home, to the same house her parents had remortgaged to pay for her college. For almost a year, she had lived like a dilettante, sleeping in too late too often and watching movies during the day. In the evenings, while her parents worked the dinner rush at their restaurant, she would often find herself walking alone along a freeway near the house.

The freeway cut through a landscape of strip malls that

all seemed to converge at one giant intersection, a collusion of Target, Starbucks, Orangetheory Fitness, the Home Depot with the notorious parking lot that had served as the scene of a shooting. She would go into these stores and buy products of little import—a box of health bars she would never eat, a tube of mascara—but that gave her an excuse to walk around. It was a time when the future could have been anything, been anywhere. It was so open that it could actually crush her. That was what she felt on those nights after graduation, especially along the stretches of freeway where the streetlights gave out.

She had offered to work at the restaurant her parents owned, but they wouldn't let her. They hadn't sent her to the University just so she could assume their livelihood, just so she could return. She had been named after Maria from *The Sound of Music*, the first film her parents had watched in America, swept up in the exploits of the nun who leaves the convent to become a governess. "Climb every mountain," the Mother Superior sings, urging Maria to leave, to see the world.

That whole sequence, the Professor informed her once, had been censored in Germany, deemed too obscene. "A nun advising a young woman to leave the convent and explore the world, the subtext being to sow her wild oats—well, it was more outrageous than any graphic scenes," he had said.

When she thought about the Professor now, she could

understand, in a way she had not before, his unhappiness in his position. She remembered, most of all, his complaints—the pressures of teaching, how little time he had to work on his next book, the bureaucratic gridlocks of the admin, the chair's short-sighted decisions, the misanthropy of certain colleagues. She could also see how, in the midst of his unhappiness, he had created the terms of their relationship. How he had encouraged her to attend his office hours, had curtailed meetings with other students to speak with her, had engaged her in emails that had nothing to do with class, and of course those naps he'd allowed her to take. Even the act of disclosing his dissatisfactions . . . All those little actions had had the effect of making her feel like the exception. positive aspect of his job, position

It was to his credit, maybe, that nothing had ever transpired between them. Maybe he had wanted her to initiate it, absolving him of liability. But she never did. She was content with the faint affect of romance, rather than its realization. By senior year, the Professor had become a little colder, more dismissive and impatient. However subtle, these changes in his demeanor were noticeable enough that she stopped going to office hours. In the absence of his attention, she was ashamed of her reliance on it. She was naïve, a clear window-pane.

And now here she was.

At a certain point, she stopped walking along the road and pivoted to return. She dropped her bouquet of collected flowers. She had been creating a mourning bouquet. But in what way was she supposed to mourn? What right did she have?

And, anyway, she had brought flowers from the chamber into her office before, arranged them in a beautiful vase, and they had decayed instantaneously in front of her, as if in a time-lapse video. What remained were moldy, phosphorous, blackened stems, water that smelled like rotting teeth. What came from that world was not meant to live in this one.

The Humanities Futures Forum began on a Saturday morning, and would last throughout the weekend. The donors filed in, wearing polo shirts and sports jackets. The lecture room was designed like a conch shell, spiraling downhill toward the speaker, who stood at its carpeted bottom, looking upward at the audience.

As everyone took their seats, the lights dimmed.

The projector turned on, and she began to speak into the microphone, welcoming them to the presentation. "Cinema, as they say, is the space of fantasy. Today, I'd like to show you clips from two films, forty years apart: *The Wizard of Oz* and *Stalker*."

The presentation screen lowered from the ceiling. A black-and-white clip from *The Wizard of Oz* played. Dorothy wakes up in her uprooted house, which has been blown away by a tornado, and the door opens onto the Land of Oz in full color. This was followed by a clip from *Stalker*, showing a group of men riding a train into the Zone. The switch again from the sepia-toned film into the full-color foliage of a new realm. → *lib hr door into a new world*

She had to remember to hold the microphone closer to her mouth. She started her sentence, then stopped and repeated it. "In each film, we journey through an alternate reality, a fantasy space, a second site—if you will—that is not of our world."

In the darkened room, she looked at the impassive faces of the audience, the wealthiest alums who were now major donors to the University. A few jotted down notes in their new University-issued notebooks and pens. HFF was technically a showcase of the University's programs, but it was mostly just classroom cosplay for them. The campus served as an elaborate set that allowed the donors to pretend they were still college students. *this girl part of community/nostalgic that*

She continued, "Whether this alternate site is called Oz *to* or the Zone, they share one similarity. The travelers within it *doh* move toward a central apparatus, a place where their wishes are said to be granted. For Dorothy and her friends, they are seeking out the Emerald City, where the Wizard resides. In *Stalker*, the travelers move toward the Room, a fabled space that will grant each passenger his subconscious wish."

Again, the screen played clips from each film. The projection showed an image of the Emerald City, followed by an image outside of the Room.

Periodically, the donors moved to the back of the room and helped themselves at the refreshments table, which was piled with finger sandwiches, cheese and crackers, fruits and canapés, buckets of champagne, an iced tea station.

She was a donor to the University too. Every season she received a routine phone call from the fundraising office, soliciting alums. She gave them her credit card number, allowed them to charge her fifty dollars. Of course, these donors must have already paid off their student loans.

She continued with her little presentation. "I can't help but observe that in each film, the protagonist never has an elaborate wish. The Stalker has guided others through the Zone many times, but has never entered the Room. And after a hard-won journey to find the Wizard, Dorothy's only wish is for a return to normalcy, a return home. Fervent, elaborate wishing, as suggested by the actions of our virtuous main characters, can only be folly."

When she was finished, she answered questions as the refreshments table was replenished by the hired catering company. Then the next group of donors came in, seated themselves. And she went through the presentation again, then held another question-and-answer session. Then the same thing. When she was done with that, another group came in. She repeated the process.

———

After the final presentation of the day, Marie understood what she had to do. She crossed the quads in the direction of Godspeed. Inside her office, she opened the closet, pushed aside the armoire, and, like many times before, disappeared into the chamber.

This time, she bypassed the road and went into the woods. It was hard to see at first, the full moon's light obscured by the foliage, by tangled tree branches. She brought out the mini flashlight on her key chain.

It wasn't as if she knew where she was going. But she followed the sound of water, which led her to a stream, glinting in the dark. Further passage into the forest was blocked by the water, which emitted a tinkling sound. Or, no, that sound wasn't water. There was something moving low to the ground, on the other side of the stream.

She stood up warily and backed up. The creature was bounding toward the bank. Reflexively, she aimed her flashlight toward it. "Oh," she said. It was a dog, thirstily lapping at the water's edge. A Bernese, collared, with jangling tags. It belonged to someone.

The dog's reflection on the water's surface was soon joined by the reflection of its owner.

She looked up. The figure was standing at a distance. It didn't shift when she shone her flashlight at it, and the beam was too weak to reveal a face. He was wearing his mackintosh and loafers, his standard dress on campus.

She glanced back at the water's surface. She was able to see a face only in the watery reflection. Was this him or a facsimile? A chimera?

She spoke, her voice tremulous and uncertain. "Professor?" she said. There was no answer. Slowly he turned and moved away, the dog by his side. She stepped closer to the stream, raised her voice this time. "Nemo?"

This time, the dog stopped and turned to look at her. It barked before catching up with its owner. Across the stream, the two figures disappeared into the woods.

It was the recurring sound of something hitting the wall, a hard clacking, that made Sean step out of his office and investigate. He had been working in Godspeed that Saturday, trying to finish an essay. The building was typically quiet on the weekends, and he'd been counting on that quiet to focus.

The door to Marie's office, just down the hall, had been left open, but she wasn't in. He stood in the doorway, glancing at her desk—which was strewn with personal items sloppily spilling out of her leather tote—before quickly stepping inside. Hesitation implied wrongdoing.

It was freezing, was the first thing he noticed. She had left the window open. The sound had been the flapping of those blinds in the wind, smacking against the frame. He closed the window. Godspeed was an old building, with a tricky heating system. Any temperature drop in one room would lower the temperature of the entire building, thus kicking the heating into overdrive and rendering all other offices even hotter. Of course, she probably hadn't considered this when she'd opened the window for that gratuitous blast of cold air. It was typical of how she moved through the world—carelessly, with short-sighted selfishness. If he brought it up to her, she would apologize only to humor him.

She must have been in the middle of something, then hurried away, leaving her belongings strewn out. On her desk, there was a phone, some extension cords, skin-care products, a burnished leather day planner. Anyone could come in and riffle through them.

He would hear her steps in the hallway if she were approaching.

This is what he was thinking when he was interrupted by the closet door opening. He glanced up just in time to see her stepping through it. "Ah, I didn't realize you were in here," he said, hiding his surprise. Then, sternly, he added, "You left the window open."

"Oh, I wasn't aware. I'm sorry." She smiled, then gestured to her open day planner in his hands. "Find anything interesting in there?"

"It fell on the floor. I was just putting it back," he lied.

"Okay," she said brightly. Whether or not she believed him, she didn't seem invested in finding out.

"You weren't here," he added unnecessarily. "Sorry, the window—"

"It's fine. Anyway, I'm off to the HFF reception." She paused, then asked, "Would you like to come with?"

"Oh, uh—I have a few things to do in the office." It might have been the first time she had ever invited him to anything.

"Are you sure? I hear there's an open bar. Donor events are always the most flush." She smiled conspiratorially.

"I know," he said stiffly.

She was gathering her things back into her tote. "Are you done with that, or?"

He looked down at her planner in his hands. "Oh, I wasn't—"

"It happens." There was no trace of suspicion in her voice.

Sean looked at her. Something was off, her lack of suspicion or irritation. He cleared his throat. Resetting the equilibrium, he said, "You should really keep the window of your office closed in the winter. It forces the heating system in the building to overcompensate, overheating everyone's offices."

She nodded. "That's right. I keep forgetting. I'll make sure to keep it shut next time." As if to herself, she said, "I should write a reminder on a Post-it."

"See that you do." He slipped out into the hallway, back to his office, where he closed the door and sat down at his desk.

He pivoted back to his laptop, the cursor blinking at him. None of the words he had just written made sense. He was very quiet for a moment as he heard her footsteps descending the staircase. From his window, he saw her leave out the front of Godspeed, her coat flapping behind her.

He got up and moved down the hall to her office again, trying the knob. As he'd anticipated, she had not set the door to self-lock. Someone like her always left a trail of oversights.

He looked around again. She had materialized out of seemingly nowhere.

He opened the closet, which felt drafty and smelled like the outdoors. Like her office, it was mostly bare, save for a piece of furniture, some kind of antique dresser. It took a moment before his eyes adjusted, and he recoiled at a blotch of black mold growing across the wall. His first instinct was to blame Marie for not having called building maintenance earlier to eradicate it. A breeze filled the closet. It took another moment before he realized it was not mold.

At first he approached the opening cautiously, ducking his head inside. He couldn't see anything. Then, unable to stop himself, he rushed through the passageway.

It did not lead to a storage space, as he had thought. He was outside. It was a clearing. He could see the silhouette of a figure standing there smoking, the back toward him. Even though he could not see the face, he knew immediately. That was her hair, the same wool coat. Was that really her, though? Who had he just seen leaving the building? He felt tricked. He hastened his steps toward her, intending to take her by surprise. "But I just saw you leave!" It was a cry both triumphant and confused. He had found her out, caught her in something—he didn't know what.

His exclamation made the figure startle. She turned around and looked at him, the cigarette falling from her mouth. It snuffed out when it hit the ground.

Peking Duck

1.

In my first years in the US, my parents take me to the library to encourage my learning of English. With my mother's guidance, I check out ten, fifteen books every weekend. Though I gravitate toward picture books, my mother pushes me toward more advanced chapter books. "Just the words themselves should be enough," she says. "If you can't think up the image on your own, then that's a failure of imagination."

This is how I come across *Iron and Silk*, recommended by a librarian as an adult book that's easy to read. It's a memoir by Mark Salzman, a wushu enthusiast who was among the first wave of Americans accepted into China in the early 1980s. He traveled to Changsha and taught English at the Hunan Medical College.

Salzman recounts how, during one lesson, he asked the

students to read aloud their essays on the topic of "My Happiest Moment." The class consisted of middle-aged teachers brushing up on their English. The last to read was Teacher Zhu, who wrote about attending a banquet dinner in Beijing years before. "First we ate cold dishes," he read, "such as marinated pig stomach and sea slugs. Then we had steamed fish, then at last the duck arrived! The skin was brown and crisp and shiny, in my mouth it was like clouds disappearing." He recounted other courses of the Peking duck dinner: eating the duck skin in pancakes with hoisin and scallions, the meat with vegetables, the duck bone soup and fruits.

At the end of his reading, Teacher Zhu set down his essay and confessed to the teacher that he never experienced this. It's someone else's memory, he said. "My wife went to Beijing and had this duck. But she often tells me about it again and again, and I think, even though I was not there, it is my happiest moment." *alma becomia portrait*

I've never had Peking duck, but it was once an image of near iconography. In a past life in Fuzhou, it represented some reality other than the one of daily congee and pickled turnips, cabbage and boiled rib soup. On TV in the evenings, I saw it in soap operas set among the wealthy, in commercials filmed in Hong Kong. When I move to the US, however, I *intuition tense* forget about it. Flipping through picture books, sometimes I conflate Peking duck with similar-looking images: a turkey from a story about the origins of Thanksgiving, the roast chicken that's part of a hallucinatory dinner spread that appears to the little match girl, foods she's fantasized about but never tasted.

2.

It's winter when I move to the US, where my parents have been living for the past few years. In the airport after we deplane, a woman lunges at me with so much excitement that I draw back toward my grandfather, my escort on the trip. The sliding doors close between us just as I recognize her, faintly, as my mother. I'm seven, and have not had a mother for two years. But I have had a grandma, whose hands, ruddy fingers inlaid with gold and jade rings, patted me reassuringly before I fell asleep at night. Next to her warm, snoring body, I drowsed on a bed overlaid with bamboo mats, keeping us cool in the subtropical heat. When it got even hotter, my grandma hung bedsheets all across the concrete balcony to block out the sun.

It's December, possibly, off the top of my memory, when I arrive. There are sensations that exist for me only in English, many associated with winter, that I experience for the first time when I move to Utah. There is the sensation of walking underneath pine trees, of wearing a too-big puffy coat, of destroying the clean surface of snow after the first snowfall, of buying discounted items in a white-tiled Osco Drug redolent of harsh cleaning chemicals, the scent of which I will always associate with being poor; overcompensatory cleanliness. The sensation of my mother dragging a wet towel across my face to clean off dried congee, and the sensation of wet skin drying in the stiff, cold air outside. We live in a one-bedroom apartment that is very clean but sometimes ants come in through the bathroom. I sleep in the living room, where, at night, I still hear my grandmother's phantom snores.

In someone else's home, a two-story mansion nestled in the mountains outside Salt Lake, a VHS cassette of *Bambi* plays on the TV while actual deer come through the backyard, pulling at the garden foliage with their teeth, and we are separated from them only by a sliding glass door.

My mother points outside. *Deer. Tree. Teeth. Eats.*

I repeat the words, then put them in sentence order: *Deer eats tree with teeth.*

The English lessons take place inside the mansion, where my mother is employed as a nanny to a toddler named Brandon. The home, which has a lobby-like foyer and elevator, is imposing enough that not even Mormon missionaries bother us. Either that, or it's too isolated from anywhere else to be worth the trek. When I first arrive in the US, my mother takes me with her to work every day, my father driving us half an hour outside the city before swinging back to campus. Inside, our days are geared around my learning English. We watch *Sesame Street*, though it's too babyish for me even then, as I learn the alphabet. I keep a daily journal and write three to five sentences in English every day.

When her charge is napping, my mother goes through ESL workbooks with me at the kitchen table, books she's found at school supply stores. One question set asks you to come up with the first letters of similar-sounding words. *Mouse, house, blouse. Pill* and *hill. Bell* and *knell. Pail* and . . . She gives me hints. "The letter you feel in your nose," she would say, and I would understand she was talking about *n*. *Nail. Pail* and *nail*. lit surrounaid on learning English

When a salesman comes to the door, he has a hard time understanding my mother. She tells him to come back later, when the owners are home, and he takes this as an invitation to come inside, to demonstrate his cleaning sprays. Peering over the railing, I think maybe he's willfully misunderstanding her, hoping it will result in a sale. My mother, noticing that I am spying, tells me to go into the other room.

I'm not sure how my mother taught me English, when her facility with the language is broken and halting. Unlike my father, she never learned English in China, and even after living in the States for years, she has never been fluent or even proficient. Cashiers at grocery stores stare at her blankly, the Mormon missionaries who show up at our apartment give up trying to convert us, and the sellers at yard sales shake their heads and over-enunciate, saying loudly, "I can't understand you." Despite this, her imperfect, broken English serves as a scaffolding for my English. still able to learn from her

The winter that I touch snow for the first time, I also taste ice cream. In the kitchen, we review the fridge and pantry foods in English. My mother names every food item, foods I've never heard of: Minute Maid orange juice concentrate, Yoplait strawberry-banana yogurt, Farley's Dinosaurs Fruit Snacks, Lay's potato chips, Surfer Cooler Capri Sun, Lunchables. I repeat each word after her. They hover in a vacuum, with no Chinese correlation. And we're not allowed to eat anything, so I can't associate word with taste.

There is, however, bing ji ling, which up until this point I have seen only on TV. My mother sneaks me some from a rectangular paper carton. Breyers French Vanilla. It's denser and sweeter than I'd expected, eggy in flavor, fuzzy with freezer burn. To my surprise, I don't like it at all and feel nauseated by its smell. But I have to like it. Because I saw ice cream on TV back home, where all my friends fantasized about how wonderful it must taste.

Ice cream is my favorite food. I write these words in the journal my mother gives me to record my first days in the US. English is just a play language to me, the words tethered to their meanings by the loosest, most tenuous connections. So it's easy to lie. I tell the truth in Chinese, I make up stories in English. I don't take it that seriously. When I'm finally enrolled in first grade, I tell classmates that I live in a house with an elevator, with deer in the backyard. It is the language in which I have nothing to lose, even if they don't believe a thing I say.

3.

During one semester of my MFA program, we begin every workshop with a discussion of a piece from *The Collected Stories of Lydia Davis*. That week's piece is called "Happiest Moment." The workshop, which takes place every Thursday evening, is held in a building typically reserved for the hotel management program. The instructor reads aloud the entirety of the story:

> If you ask her what is a favorite story she has written, she will hesitate for a long time and then say it may be this story that she read in a book once: an English language teacher in China asked his Chinese student to say what was the happiest moment in his life. The student hesitated for a long time. At last he smiled with embarrassment and said that his wife had once gone to Beijing and eaten duck there, and she often told him about it, and he would have to say the happiest moment of his life was her trip, and the eating of the duck.

The instructor looks at the class, eight students scattered around a conference table in a fluorescently lit seminar room. "So, what do we think?"

We talk about the way the story frames and reframes an

anecdote. Thom, whom everyone calls "the plot Nazi," likens this device to a game of telephone, as the story is transmitted from person to person. "The wife tells her husband the story about eating Peking duck, the husband shares the story with the teacher, laying claim to it as his own happiness, the teacher writes a book incorporating this story. And then, in this piece, the writer describes what she read in a book, which is recounted by the narrator. It's being reframed once again."

We talk about the reframing and what we think it's trying to achieve. I tell them of *Iron and Silk*, which contains the same anecdote. "This story doesn't give credit to the Salzman memoir, but I can't imagine that it *isn't* a reference to that book."

Matthew, the only other Asian student in our program, has read the book too. He says, "This idea of framing and reframing the same anecdote raises a question: Can the writer, who's retelling another's story, really assume authorship? And, going along those lines, can Mark Salzman assume authorship for his student's story?"

We kick this ball around for a bit, discussing the difference between appropriating someone's story and making it new through retelling, without drawing much of a conclusion. At some point Allie declares, "By writing the story, the writer naturally lays claim to it." To which Matthew responds, "But we know that's just an excuse. Authorial license never justifies appropriation."

In the ensuing silence, the instructor smiles. "Well, these are all great points," she says smoothly. "Since we're running out of time, we need to get started with workshop." She turns to me. "Let's begin with your story."

4.

My workshop story follows a Chinese immigrant nanny through the span of a Friday, when she brings her young daughter to the mansion where she is employed. The piece is written from the nanny's perspective, as she moves through a seemingly ordinary workday, interrupted only by the arrival of a door-to-door salesman, who persistently tries to sell her cleaning products. The day culminates in her losing her job once the parents return home from work. Her daughter observes the proceedings.

"Well," the instructor says brightly. "This is a very interesting story. Let's open up discussion. Any thoughts?"

Thom always speaks first. "The way English is rendered in this piece, it's kind of artificial. I mean, the first-person narration reads too smoothly and is too well articulated for a non-English-speaking protagonist."

Others in workshop echo some of Thom's sentiments about the inherent clumsiness of rendering the experiences of a non–English speaker in English, but there's no consensus on how to solve this issue. Someone suggests that it could be written in Chinglish instead, but another student counters that this would play into stereotypes. "Using Chinglish would exaggerate the character's inarticulateness, and flatten her into an immigrant trope."

From the far end of the conference table, Matthew clears his throat. Somehow, I've been waiting for his response. "Whether the story is written in English or Chinglish," he says deliberately, "it's just a tired Asian American subject, these stories about immigrant hardships and, like, intergenerational woes."

I can't look at Matthew. His thesis is a Western novel that, in his words, interrogates white masculinity. The few times we've spoken outside of class, he's talked mostly about his summers in Taiwan, which he spends playing basketball with his cousins. He continues, "It also doesn't help that this is a stereotypical representation of a female Chinese immigrant."

There is an awkward silence. Now it's the instructor who clears her throat. "For those of us who may not be familiar, can you expand on this stereotype, Matthew?"

I look at him.

"Yeah," he says. "Like, when the salesman just invites himself inside, she just goes along with it. She's very passive. It fits into these representations of these meek, submissive women we see all the time. It's unrealistic." He doubles down. "It's a kind of Asian *minstrelsy*."

When no one wants to speak, Thom does. "Is this story autobiographical?"

"The writer isn't allowed to answer during workshop," Allie points out.

There is another lull in the room.

"Well, I found the story *so* interesting," the instructor interjects, forced cheer in her voice. "It shows how these differences in cultural assimilation, in English fluency, can alienate this immigrant mother and daughter from each other." Her voice rises. "And then there are these *startling* moments of tenderness . . ."

5.

My mother drinks only water in restaurants; any other drink order is an unnecessary expenditure. Because she is my mother, I do the same and order water, even though she's long ago given up on lecturing me about frugality. A few weeks before my book release, I take her out to a fancy Chinese restaurant, a half-empty banquet hall with roast ducks hanging in the front window. The restaurant is famed for its Peking duck, which is ranked the second best in the world, according to a travel magazine.

When the waiter comes, I order for us, in English, the usual dishes. "So, we'll get B16, C7, and F22. To start, we'd like A5 and A11."

My mother sets her menu down, looks at me. "Is that how you order? Like a computer."

"Okay, sounds good." The waiter, a Chinese teenager in Air Force 1s, also answers in English. "I'll get those appetizers out first."

Before the dishes arrive, I give her an advance copy of my book, a story collection with a vaguely Chinese cover image of persimmons in a Ming dynasty bowl. "It comes out next month."

"So this is the final copy? I'll show your father when I return." She studies it skeptically, like a lottery ticket that will never yield, frowning at the marketing copy on the jacket flap. "Haven't these stories been published already?"

"Some have. They're just all collected in one book."

"They can just read them for free somewhere else?"

"Have you read any of them already?"

"I looked at the story about the nanny you sent me." She slides the book into her purse. "So, where do you get your ideas?" She asks this in a lightly mocking tone, pretending to be an interviewer.

"For the nanny story? Well, obviously based on your job long ago."

Though we start off speaking English, all conversations with my mother eventually move toward Mandarin, the language in which she is the most agile, darting insults and embedding her observations with acid subtext. Though I am no longer fluent in Mandarin, I try to accommodate. Her English is awkward and mangled, and it's not easy to move through the world shielded from the unkindness of others only by their thin veneer of liberal respectability.

The teenage waiter returns with appetizers and main dishes together, setting down mock-chicken bean curd, lotus root, garlic pea shoots, mapo tofu, and salt and pepper smelt sprinkled with tiny diced jalapeños. It's all coming out so quickly, making me wonder about the quality. Topping off our water, he asks, "Is there anything else I can get you?"

Not bothering to switch back to English, my mother asks for a little side dish of chili bamboo.

"I'm sorry, what?" he says.

"A2," I tell him, and he rushes away. My mother helps herself delicately to a bite of pea shoots, then the smelt. "Do you think the food is good here?"

"I like simple food," she says, neither confirming nor denying. Maybe it was ridiculous to come to a restaurant famed for its Peking duck and just order regular dishes. Neither of us like duck though, its fatty skin. She pretends to correct herself. "No, no, that's wrong. What I *should* say is: I love it, honey! This is the best."

"But you would never say that."

She smiles her Cheshire grin. "But I don't want to be like the usual Chinese mother, someone who is never satisfied, yells at their children, and keeps saying *ai-yah* all the time."

Now I understand. "Do you think it's you in these stories?"

"There are so many mothers in your stories, what am I supposed to think?" My mother is suddenly indignant. "But they're all so miserable. Does there have to be so much suffering?"

I look down at my plate, a mound of rice covered with gushy mapo. "Well, they're not all about you. I wasn't trying to capture your experience."

"You weren't trying to capture my experience," she repeats, as if to herself. "Then why did you write them?"

I'm surprised by this question. "Well, the nanny story was more based on you, compared to the others. It was about what happened to us when you worked as a nanny. I wanted to show how terrible—"

"But how would you even know what happened? It happened to *me*, not to us. You were too young to understand. And you weren't in the room. I made sure of that."

"I was in the hall, listening. And you told me when I was older. The details were very disturbing."

My mother is smiling incongruously. "But, see, you're not tough. You need to be tough. He was just a silly man. You made him seem almost dangerous."

"He *was* dangerous, very unpredictable. He was nice one moment, then scary the next. The things he said to you, they were very hurtful."

She sighs a little. "Look, we're not like Americans. We don't need to talk about everything that gives us a negative feeling. I wouldn't move forward if I just kept thinking about it. But I do move forward. I set a good example for you. And you had a great childhood."

I take a sip of water. We've been over this before. There's no point in setting the record straight for the millionth time about my childhood, the school bullying. The worst part was how my mother used to encourage me to lie to her, to pretend how great things were. She would phrase her questions like "You're popular at school, right?" or "You have a lot of friends, right?," priming me to answer the way she wanted. She couldn't not have known that I was lying, but she wanted to bathe in the lies. She needed to believe I was thriving in the US, that my happiness came at the cost of hers, rather than acknowledge the fact that we were both miserable in this country together. *bc thin can be doing it for somion?*

Instead of arguing this time, I simply say, "My therapist says that it is always better to acknowledge reality."

She flinches at my mention of therapy, which, predictably, closes the conversation. As we pick at our food in silence, I hear the sound of the TV playing a compilation reel of food show segments that feature the restaurant. In one clip, the host tells the audience that Peking duck goes as far back as the fourteenth century. He looks at the viewer, breaking the fourth wall. "So remember, when you take a bite of that mouthwatering barbecue, you're eating a piece of history."

The waiter comes. "How is everything?"

"Great. I think we're actually going to get the rest of this boxed up," I tell him.

My mother turns to him. In Mandarin, she gives elaborate instructions on how she wants the leftovers wrapped so that I can take them home.

He waits for her to finish, then smiles in embarrassment. "I'm sorry, I don't speak Chinese."

6.

I am making lunch for the children when the doorbell rings. Because the owners' house is in a remote area outside Salt Lake, it's unusual that we receive guests. Sometimes I ignore the doorbell when there is someone outside, the same way I ignore phone calls to the house. Let them go to the answering machine or leave a note. They're not here to talk to me.

But today I feel restless. I take the elevator down to the large foyer, where I open the door.

"Good afternoon!" It's a man carrying a clipboard and a caddy of cleaning products. "I just have one question. How clean would you say your home is?" He holds up the cleaning spray, and informs me that I can take it today for a one-week trial, and if I like it, there's an installment plan for the entire set . . . His enthusiasm makes him speak very quickly and I can't catch everything. "Just try it for a week! And then I can come back in seven days to see what you think."

In his jeans and plaid shirt, he doesn't look like a salesman. His long dirty-blond hair and goatee aren't well-groomed, either. He's looking at me, then past me, at the gleaming, tiled foyer, which amplifies our voices, the elevator leading up to the second floor, the upstairs railing. He's taking everything in.

now from mother's perspective

"No, thank you. I'm not the owner." I smile politely.

He hesitates. "So are you the cleaning lady?"

"I work here. I don't clean." I don't feel the need to specify that I'm the nanny, looking after two children, my daughter and a charge named Brandon. "You come back later. The owners come home. Maybe they buy."

"Oh, okay." After a pause, he resumes. "This product works for everyone, though. It can go on all surfaces. Let me show you." He walks past me, into the foyer, and begins cleaning the wooden bench next to the elevator.

I worked for a cleaning company when I first came to the States. During the training, the manager told us trainees to crouch down when we are wiping floors with a rag. And then he looked at us, all these women cleaning on their hands and knees. Why would we not use mops and brooms? I'm not a dog, so I quit.

The man in front of me kneels to polish the legs of the bench, and soon he is on all fours. It's strange that he doesn't at least feel shame in this position, a position he voluntarily assumes. Maybe he wants me to feel sorry for him. "Very nice. It's very good," I tell him. "Maybe we buy later."

He looks up. "They don't sell this in stores, ma'am!" When the elevator comes—had he pressed the button?—and opens its doors, he walks inside, spraying down the metal handrail, the two-button panel. Unsure of what to do, I step inside with him. There is dirt under his nails, and his clothes carry the smell of gasoline, making me think of farming equipment. The elevator feels very small with two people. He asks, "What are you up to today?"

"It's very busy day. I make lunch now."

"Well, I could use some lunch too." He smiles at me. When the doors open, he steps out, marveling at the rest of the home, its view of the valley and mountains below. It's good that my daughter is not within sight, is in another room. And Brandon, whom the man does not notice, is still sleeping on the sofa.

I follow him, a bit helplessly.

"I haven't eaten all day." He seats himself at the kitchen table, sliding my coupons off so they fall to the floor. It's when he looks at me, a kind of leer on his face, that I finally realize the situation has become unusual. "So, what kind of Chinese food can you cook me?"

"I don't cook Chinese food," I say, somewhat formally.

"Come on, play along." It is his first sign of impatience. "What about moo shu?"

"Mushrooms?" I know what he means.

"No, moo shu. It's a dish. It's listed on all those menus."

"Oh. I don't know." I shake my head.

He is annoyed. "Come on, now. I'm not asking for the real thing. I'm asking for you to play along."

"I don't eat moo shu where I am from in China," I say calmly, and that seems to placate him. Of the two of us, only I can be the expert on this. Before he gets too angry, however, I tell him, "I can make egg and tomato."

He hesitates. "Is that like egg foo young?"

"No, egg and tomatoes. I stir-fry with rice wine and sugar." It is my favorite quick dinner.

"That doesn't sound too good." After a pause, he says, "What about Peking duck?"

"I don't have duck. But how about kung fu chicken?" I am just making up names.

He hesitates. "Okay," he finally says.

"This is *real* Chinese cooking," I warn him. As for what kung fu chicken is, I don't know. I wanted to say wushu chicken.

In the fridge, there is a leftover roast chicken. I shred the white meat with my hands, afraid of using a knife and revealing where all the sharp objects might be. I make a soy-oil-sugar marinade, then stir-fry the chicken with some green onions, which I also tear apart into jagged pieces. The result is maybe a terrible stir-fry version of three-cup chicken. What matters is that it passes as Chinese to his taste.

There is a wall phone in the kitchen. I calculate the risk of calling 911, but decide against it. It's too obvious. He'll see me. According to the clock, it is two forty-five in the afternoon. The parents, who co-own a Mormon jewelry company, usually get home early on Fridays, around three. All I need to do is distract him for the fifteen or twenty minutes until they return.

"This is good," he says, after taking the first few bites, and I feel sorry for him that he can't tell that what I've cooked is actually a mess, sprinkled heavily with a dusty five-spice bottle, using old soy sauce packets I found in a drawer of takeout menus. I wouldn't serve it to anyone I cared about. And he thinks it's good. I almost wish I had made it better.

Then he puts his arm around my waist, and I stiffen. "This is all I want, you know?"

"You want some tea?" I move beyond his reach.

"I want beer. You got any beer?" Feeling bolder, he gets up and begins to root through the fridge himself. My daughter peeks into the doorway of the kitchen, a little confused. Irritably, I gesture for her to hide herself, and she does.

"I get it for you!" I pretend to scold him, which he seems to like. "Finish the food."

He sits back down. "Yes, ma'am." We are playing house, I realize, like the way my daughter plays it with the Taiwanese boy next door. She brushes the doorway with a pretend broom and scolds him for tracking dirt into the house. He pretends to watch TV and acts grouchy.

When I place a cold can before him, he tells me to pour it into a tall glass. As I do this, he tells me earnestly, "I can take you away from here." He points out the window, to an indeterminate spot in the distance. "I live in a cabin, out there in the woods."

Where he's pointing, all I see is a row of snowcapped mountains. I often sit here alone, while the kids are watching TV, and look out the triangular window, built to frame the steeple. It is my favorite part of the house, with a view of the sunset in the late afternoons. I can estimate the time of day by the way the light looks. Sometimes I think the landscape of Utah is the most beautiful I have ever seen. This view may be the only thing that anchors me to this job, to this new life my husband insists on pursuing.

The man says, in a voice low and wistful, "Do you want to come with me?"

"I will think about it," I say, as if deciding whether to buy his cleaning sprays. I feel more afraid than I sound. "I'm very busy. People rely on me." It's all so logical. I stop short of filling in the details. That my husband is a PhD student in math, in his second year. That he is paid a small stipend. Until he graduates, I work to help support the family. I went through a string of jobs before landing at this one, the most leisurely one, the one that feels like passing time more than all the others. I am almost thirty-five years old.

"Oh. That's a pity." He looks down at his beer. His voice changes. "But I'm going to be honest. When people see you, they can tell you don't belong here." He rushes into his next sentence. "Now, I'm not trying to offend you, and you know how you're different, the way you look and talk. You're obviously not from here."

"Hmm." I pretend to consider this.

He taps on the window, indicating his home in the distance. "But where I live, it's far away from anyone. And I'm completely self-sufficient, you'll see. I have a water pump, I have my own electricity. There's no one around to judge me." He turns to me. "So, do you think you'll reconsider?"

"I don't think so."

"Well, why the hell not?" His agitation is a little splash of hot oil.

"Do you know what I used to do in China?" I say, looking out the window. Not at anything in particular, the trees and mountains and the road winding through them, carrying, in the distance, the mother's car, painted a shiny beige shade that I think of as champagne. She will be home soon.

Maybe it's because of the sight of that car, knowing someone is coming, that I tell this man more than I would normally, more than I've ever told my employers. How, in another life, I worked at an accounting firm, where I managed the accounts of the mayor and other prominent local officials. There weren't as many high-rise buildings then, but our office was located in one, and we worked on one of the upper levels. I made more money than my husband, whom I was only dating then. During the years of reeducation, he wrote me long, impassioned letters, a passion I never sensed from him in person. He, along with both my sisters, had been sent out into the countryside to work for years. Hard labor, manual labor. I saw their hands when they returned. But not me. I stayed in the city because of my job, which was deemed crucial to the party. I stayed in the city and looked after my parents. Sometimes it felt as if I were one of the few young adults who lived there. I liked that time very much, when everything else—marriage, children—was something that had been planned but nothing I had to think about in the day-to-day. I liked knowing my life was following a track without having to accept the responsibility of it.

When I'm done, I turn away from the window. Who knows how much he even understood of what I've said? At some point, I had lapsed into Mandarin. I can't communicate the complicated things in English.

"So, are you a communist?" he asks, looking at me curiously.

I know there's no answer except no. "No."

"Good, because we don't like communists in this country. You know what we do with them?" I can't tell if he's joking. I've always thought those old American movies about the Cold War were just movies. He stands up, his face a scowl. "Do you know what we do with communists?"

I don't say anything, silenced with fear I don't want to admit. Looking past him, I see my daughter standing in the doorway again. I am filled, suddenly, irrevocably, with anger. "Get out of here," I tell her in Chinese. "Go, go into the other room." When she doesn't move, I raise my voice to a scream. "Get out!" I yell, and she rushes away.

The sound of the garage door opening fills the room.

———

When my daughter first came to the States, she would insist that I tell her a bedtime story every night before sleep. This was a tradition her grandma established when she lived in China without me. So I tried to make up stories, simple fables with a moral lesson. Except when we came to the end, my mind would go blank. What's the lesson here supposed to be? I would always lose track, thinking she'd be asleep long before the story finished. But she would wait for the conclusion, and if it didn't satisfy her, she would ask a lot of questions. She wanted the story to make sense, at a time when my own life didn't make any sense. Shortly after, I began taking her to the library. I would read her picture books instead, and that solved my problem with thinking up the endings.

The ending of what happened that day is that as soon as he hears the garage door opening, the salesman panics. Cursing me, he stands up quickly, the fork and knife dashing off the table. Watching him rush out the door and then downstairs, I think, This is so easy. This problem of this stupid stranger is so easily solved despite all the fear I'd felt.

Then the wife comes through the garage door. She looks at the messy kitchen, the cutlery that scattered across the floor as he'd bolted up to leave. I explain everything, relieved. Then she asks me a lot of questions. Questions like: Did you invite him inside? Did he misunderstand, maybe, your English? Why didn't you ask him to leave? Did you offer him food? When he forced you to cook food for him, why didn't you just say no? Why is there beer open in the kitchen? Did he also force you to give him a beer? What made you afraid of him? Did he have a weapon on him? How did the food get all over the place?

I'm answering her as well as I can, but in the middle of my answers, she interrupts with another question. And so my English falters, becomes distracted and nervous. When she can't fully understand my responses, she looks to my daughter, who is only too eager to translate.

My husband, who has arrived to pick us up, watches intently from the kitchen doorway.

The mother says, more to herself, "I have to figure out what to do."

"What about calling the police?" my husband suggests.

"Well, it's tricky, given the situation we have worked out." She trails off.

"We're legal US residents," he says, thinking he's clarifying.

But I know what she's referring to. Even though we have our green cards, I'm not their legal employee, and they pay me under the table. "Let me talk it over with Dave when he gets home," she finally says. "He should be getting back any minute." She glances at the clock, then at me. Indicating the mess of food all over the kitchen, she asks, "Well, can you clean this up now? Then you can go."

"No." It's a reflex, how quickly I say this.

"What do you mean?" She's looking at me. Does she really think I'm going to drop everything to clean her kitchen? While my husband and daughter look on?

"She wants you to clean up, Mom," my daughter says in Chinese. She thinks I can't understand.

I look at my husband. I want him to intervene, to defend me. He opens his mouth, then closes it, unsure. He is an agreeable person, but his problem is that he wants to please everyone. That's how you survive here, he told me. But just because he wants to live in this country doesn't mean I have to eat shit.

She purses her lips. "But that's your job."

"No. I take care of Brandon." All the times that I've wiped down the countertops, the stove, the inside of the microwave at their request—I have tried to be a good employee, going above and beyond, but cleaning is not actually part of my job. They pay me less than what a trained nanny would cost, what a maid would cost.

She doesn't say anything for a moment. "Someone has to clean up. And I didn't make this mess," she says, not looking at me.

I don't say anything.

"I'll do it," my daughter announces, grabbing the paper towels. I yank her arm back, and she yells in pain.

"Maybe you can talk about it on Monday," my husband proposes.

"Bye, Brandon," I tell him as he squeezes his warm body against mine. I give him a little hug. I am not coming back on Monday, I decide. Maybe that will turn out to be a lie, but it's a lie I need in this moment. Without looking at anyone, I go out the front door and sit in the passenger seat of the car, waiting.

It is several minutes before my husband and my daughter come to the driveway. "You shouldn't have done that," he says, grimacing as he gets into the driver's seat and starts the engine. We drive downhill. My daughter chimes in from the back seat, "Brandon's mom is very nice, Mom. She just wants to know what happened."

In the rearview mirror, I study my daughter. When I first learned I was having a daughter, the family was so disappointed. In China, a boy is always better, if you're going to have one child. But me, I was secretly happy. A boy, at best, can adore his mother, but a girl can understand her. When the doctor told me it was a girl, I thought, Now I will be understood. That was my happiest moment. The idea of a daughter.

"Don't talk to me about things you don't understand," I tell her now.

She blinks, doesn't say anything. She makes herself very quiet, as she should, and looks out the window. Good, I think. Don't look at me.

As if by instinct, she looks up. Our eyes meet in the mirror. Then she looks away.

Tomorrow

After the final throes of the relationship—the aimless arguments about the future, the listless waiting for his circular non–decision making, the studying of feminist tracts to recondition herself—she did not come away with nothing. She came away with a baby, which was still forming. It had been a surprise; she'd thought herself past childbearing age. That, and her IUD, which had become so deeply embedded in her uterine lining that only the uninsured process of surgical extraction could remove it, had created a false narrative of childlessness. She had not counted on the device to actually expire.

Because she was estranged from her body, she did not confirm the pregnancy until it became too risky to reverse anything. A boy. She notified the father. In light of their breakup, it was up to her, he emphasized, what she wanted to do. She didn't know, she barely had time to think. "Well, you need some time to think. Treat yourself to a weekend away. When was the last time you left DC?" he'd asked, and she realized that it had been eleven years. On impulse, she bought a flight to Miami.

She used up some vacation days and ate imitation crab-meat by the sea. The tides ebbed and flowed. The baby moved in concert with them. She knew she would keep it. This re-alization was not met with celebratory feeling so much as obsessive accounting of her financial health. Could she even afford it? These were the liquefiable assets at hand: a draw-erful of family jewelry, a 401(k), an IRA, and a one-bedroom condo purchased with inheritance money after her parents' passing.

At the beach, a floating island of trash washed ashore, the frothing waves spewing plastic debris, bottles, tampon appli-cators, dental floss across the sand. The beachgoers gathered up their personal items and scattered, complaining about how long it would take the park staff to clean up. She took her towel and retreated to the hotel.

This was a different, if not an inevitable, time. The US was no longer number one. The "recyclable" waste of other na-tions was shipped here instead. Migrants no longer rushed its borders. Countries had begun programs of de-Americanizing, severing ties with US companies and businesses, and levying fines and taxes in trade. Its most significant cultural artifacts, including the Constitution, the Declaration, were on loan to foreign museums, displayed in clumsily curated exhibitions that lumped them with British curios.

The question of how to raise a child in this time and place.

If the baby's father were here, he would have said, "Is this a local issue or a global issue?" A local issue, according to his definition, was a contained problem with an identifiable solution. A global issue was a problem created by a complex, undefined causal network, and therefore had no definitive solution. For that reason, a global issue was not worth worrying about. "If you just ask yourself, Local or global?, half your problems will disappear." Was it a wilted salad or was it climate change? Was it a poorly developed war movie or was it our colonial mindset?

It was unfortunate that during her only vacation in years, she continued to think about him. She wished he would contact her; her grief was such that she looked for him in dreams. Was this local or global?

In the hotel lobby, the speakers played a languid folk song covered by Nina Simone, "Black Is the Color of My True Love's Hair." It flowed over her. *Yes, I love the ground on where he goes. And still I hope . . .* Only then did she realize she had always misheard the lyrics as "Black is the color of my true love's heart."

It was in the bathroom of her hotel room that, while undressing, she made a puzzling discovery. Removing the linen tunic over her bathing suit, she noticed a protrusion between her legs. She took off the suit and looked at her body in the large mirror.

"Oh my god."

It was an appendage of ruddy flesh. It was coming out of her vagina. She touched it. It seemed to shrink from her touch, though it did not completely dart back inside. It was, well, an arm. No larger than the size of a Sharpie. The skin was pink. No, the skin was translucent, and the flesh underneath was pink, marbled with tiny, fragile veins that looked like they would bruise if she so much as sneezed. There were . . . fingers, somewhat webbed. It was a baby arm.

Was she going into labor? But her water had not broken.

Moving carefully, she began to dial 911, but then stopped herself. Was this local or global? She was not in pain. She would have to dip into her savings to call an ambulance to the ER, since most ambulance providers didn't take insurance. She examined the arm again, flexing it at the elbow. (Should she have washed her hands first?) It shivered a little, as if cold. It was alive. It did not, to the best of her assessment, appear to be in pain. And if she herself was not in pain (was she?), then it must not be an emergency. An emergency was an emergency only if you called it that by name.

At the immediate-care clinic, she filled out a form with her personal info. A kindly nurse examined her, then transmitted the findings to the doctor, who stepped into the room only after the exam was over. "So, Eve," the doctor said, studying her chart, "the good news is that you're not going into labor. Your water hasn't broken. The arm seems to be stopping it."

She swallowed. "Will the baby be okay?"

"Well, geriatric pregnancies in general are higher risk. But the ultrasound shows no irregularities. Its heart rate is normal—very robust, actually." He paused. "I know this is an unusual situation. But I've seen this before, and the situation is relatively safe for the baby, just delicate. You'll want to re-strict your movements."

"Yes, but . . . the arm is just sticking out." Eve gestured vaguely to her nether region, covered by the paper gown. It took effort not to feel embarrassed. It was only her body, one of many he looked at every day.

"I'm aware," he said. He did not wish to look at it. Preg-nancy deformities were not as uncommon as patients seemed to think. Some said it was from microplastics in the water, from discontinued feminine hygiene products, from asbestos-laced talcum powder. All lawsuits had been settled out of court. "For the remainder of the pregnancy," he explained, "one part of the baby will grow outside the womb rather than inside. It's not ideal, but I've seen worse."

She looked at him in disbelief. "But will the arm develop like the rest of the body if it's . . . outside the womb?"

"You say it's his right arm?" He consulted the file.

"Yes."

"Well, he might not grow up to be a pitcher." He looked up from the files. "Are you a baseball fan?"

"Um, not really."

"Ha, yeah." He smiled noncommittally. "Well, it's an American thing. Maybe you have to grow up with it."

Eve nodded blankly. Why would he assume she had not grown up with it? Why wouldn't he assume that she was a second- or third-generation immigrant? Already she was giving this more thought than he had. She changed the subject. "So will his arm be okay?"

"Yes, probably." He explained the mechanics. The arm would continue to grow, but at a slower rate than the wombed body. It would always be underdeveloped, a forever-convalescent limb. "There aren't a lot of studies done on this. I would say the best thing to do is just to observe its movements. Often it will hang limp as the fetus is resting. But as you enter the second and third trimesters, the arm will begin to show more movement. If it's uncomfortable or perturbed, you'll know. Don't be afraid to engage with it. If it's doing something you don't like, don't be afraid to correct its positioning. Gently, of course."

She nodded again. "So how do I take care of this arm with . . . synthetic measures?"

"Let me just check . . ." He looked at some things on the desktop, pulling up what looked like WebMD. "So it says here: Just make sure the arm is comfortable, not twisted at odd angles. Be careful how you sit. Keep it warm. You can put oil on it. There's a website that sells fetal-limb warmers for this, and lotions too." He looked around for his prescription pad to write down the URL.

"Is there anything else?" She was worried she would forget everything.

"Actually, yes!" As if he'd just remembered. "With this type of complication, the pregnancy often extends past full term. It's unclear why. You'll likely carry longer than forty weeks, could be fifty, even. We don't have effective methods of giving an estimate. You should follow up with your obstetrician."

"Do you have a pamphlet or something?" Her focus was dissolving. "I'm sorry, I'm not going to remember all this. I . . ." She wanted to cry. Searching for further questions, she asked, "What about when I have to pee?"

His flinch was so slight that it could only have been imagined. "Yes, we haven't gotten to the part about bodily logistics, have we?" He smiled. "When you urinate, make sure to wipe the arm down afterward. Urine is a sterile substance, so it shouldn't become infected if you take care of it correctly." He consulted the clock on the wall. "I'll let you get dressed. The front desk will take your co-pay."

"Okay." Instead of crying, she sneezed. When she sneezed, she could feel the arm shake, its jiggly, vibrational energy. "At least it's only the arm," she said, as if to herself.

Shutup

"Atta girl," the doctor said, which was an insane thing to say. She must've misheard. It was probably something like *There you go* instead.

She put on a long, billowy dress and strolled down Ocean Drive, swaying a little to music emitted by nightclubs across the street. The baby arm swung lightly, a cherubic pendulum. She slowed her gait, not wanting to jostle it further. Along the boardwalk, beachgoers played volleyball, even at this late hour. Older women seemed to smile at her as they walked past. Her first instinct was to check whether the baby arm was visible, but she realized they were just smiling at her belly. She was identifiably pregnant.

When friends used to ask her if she wanted to start a family, she would eschew the question by saying, "The economy doesn't support it." Which wasn't entirely justifiable. People with lesser means had children. Everyone expected to die in debt, and had learned not to mind. It was just a fact of living in a country on the decline.

For the last eleven years, Eve had worked for the Image and Reputation Office of the US government. The office monitored the country's standing in other places, compiling reports based on foreign news articles, blog posts, and social media mentions into one big-data document every quarter. They alerted the Pentagon to extremist threats.

As protocol for any government job, she'd had to submit

to an FBI background check and questioning before the official hire. An agent had asked about her relationship to her home country. "Please describe," he'd instructed, reading from a form, "the loyalties, if any, that you feel toward your non-US place of origin."

"I feel sympathy and goodwill toward its people and its culture," she'd said carefully, "but not toward its government."

"Okay, great." The FBI agent had written something down, then moved on to more detailed questions. She had disclosed all the facts: That she had immigrated to the US when she was six. That the last time she had visited her home country was in college, when her parents were still alive. "But you still have family there?" he'd asked.

"Well, most of my family back home have moved away to other countries." Maybe she shouldn't have referred to it as "home." She added, "There's no reason to visit now."

"You must miss them," he'd surmised, the empathy in his voice a mislead. He was deducing her loyalties.

She deferred his probing by offering more facts. "There's a great-aunt who still lives there. I didn't know her very well. I don't have many memories of her." The great-aunt was the last of the older generation who had stayed.

She remembered the last time she had visited her home city, sitting around in various relatives' living rooms and socializing at big family banquets. She had mostly kept to herself, except when her grandmother addressed her with edicts about marrying before she turned into a "leftover" at twenty-seven, and how she needed to have a child before thirty. Her father didn't like to leave her alone with relatives. She had thought he was being protective before realizing, some years after his death, that, actually, he had been ashamed—of her faulty language skills and colloquialisms, her blunt American mannerisms, her lack of cultural savvy, the way she dressed. So American.

She had blabbed some of this to the FBI agent, amplifying her ambivalence. In the end, she had been hired.

It was dark by the time Eve reached the southernmost end of Miami Beach. Past the beach, there was a long concrete pier that extended into the ocean. She walked out onto it. The tip of America, though not the limit of its once-empiric sweep. In the dark, the ocean was a self-vomiting mass that could be heard but not seen. The waves emitted a thirsty slurp. Floating in oceans beyond, America's countless former territories: Puerto Rico, the Philippines, Guam, the Virgin Islands, Saipan . . .

I should just leave, she thought, staring out into the dark. What she meant by that, she wasn't sure. She needed to put some distance between herself and the baby's father, that was for sure. But something else, something unspoken.

When her parents passed a few years ago, she had felt relief at finally being freed of their expectations. They were her only family living in the States. Yet by that point she could no longer conceive of a life beyond the one they had envisioned for her. Her habits had already calcified. So she continued on as they had wished, holding her job as a government functionary. Even having a baby would have been in keeping with what they had wanted.

If there was one deviation she could allow herself . . . She wanted to leave this country, a place her parents idolized as the land of opportunity. Coming here, for them, had been the grand ambition, the only dream. But now their only child had the thought of returning, of a homecoming.

In that moment, a gust of wind swept across the pier, a breeze at first, until it grew more insistent. The baby arm contracted. It felt as if it were trying to pull itself out of her. This hurt wildly, a foreshadowing of contractions. When the wind died down, she lifted up the hem of her dress, and she saw that the arm was pointing, its index finger extended toward the ocean, the darkness. She took that as a sign.

She petted the vibrating limb through the fabric of her skirt, trying to steady its tense, frantic energy. "Okay, we will go," she conceded, and it was a long moment before the arm relaxed.

On the red-eye return flight to DC, she looked out the window as the plane prepared for landing, at all the usual landmarks: the Washington Monument, the Pentagon, the BioPark. DC was basically a company town, flanked by other company towns. On the Virginia side was the defense industry, on the Maryland side the pharmaceutical industry. She was often very lonely. As the plane lowered, the geography became more defined, more inescapable.

She went straight from the airport to the office. It was like any Monday morning. Adjusting her skirt as she sat down at her desk, she was careful not to sit on the baby arm. From the messages in her inbox, it seemed that most coworkers were not even aware she had been on vacation.

"Eve, can you come with me?" It was her boss, standing at the entry to her cubicle.

Inside his office, she did not sit down. She stood there, looking out the window behind his desk. The view overlooked Lafayette Square, and beyond that, the back of the White House. From behind, it looked like any other building.

He did not sit either, but leaned against his desk, facing her. "How was your vacation?" he asked carefully.

"Fine. It gave me time to reflect." She paused. "I've decided that it would probably be best if I no longer worked here."

He tsked, involuntarily. "Don't do that."

"Don't do what?"

He clasped his hands. He was a deliberate man, lean and business-casual handsome. "This isn't the first time you've wanted to quit."

"Ben." She spoke slowly. "I don't want the complications of working in the same office as my ex-boyfriend, who also happens to be my boss." Although *ex-boyfriend* was a stretch for their noncommittal, on-off relations.

"Have you thought that, given your situation, this would be the worst time to lose a job?"

"I have reserves," she said, with too much dignity.

"What about health insurance?"

She almost rolled her eyes. "Look, you can either lay me off or I can quit."

"But I don't have any reason to let you go."

"Isn't there always a budgetary issue at this time of the year?" she hinted.

"Let's just . . . slow down here." He looked tired, older than his years. They were the same age, had started in this department at the same time, but he had advanced more quickly than she. He was not a natural manager; being forced to make decisions that affected others made him break out in hives. For Secret Santa two years before, she had gifted him a bottle of calamine lotion. Though it had been a joke, his gratitude had taken her aback. They'd started dating in the dead week between Christmas and New Year's, if a lunch break in a deserted office qualified as a date.

She sat down on the sofa. "It's going to be a lot of childcare. All I see in front of me is work and more work." She did not look at him as she said these things. "If I don't take a break now, I won't have the chance to do so again for a while."

"So what you want is not necessarily to quit. You want to

take a leave, maybe an extended vacation." He was always willfully misinterpreting her. "We were supposed to take a vacation together," he said, almost to himself.

"Sure." Eve didn't want to rehash their broken plans. At one point, they had planned on traveling overseas together, for a tour through parts of Asia. But since his idea of a good time was touring Civil War battlefields, she should have seen that he would eventually back out. Someone who found eating pad thai too "challenging" probably wouldn't adapt to traveling so far afield.

Things made sense when Eve met his new girlfriend, who had once stopped by the office to pick Ben up. They were on their way to a clambake, a Friday night with friends at the marina. Wearing a kelly green tennis dress with white espadrilles, she was carrying a sheet cake resembling a flag, blueberries and strawberries as the stars and stripes arranged across a layer of whipped cream. Seeing the two of them together in the doorway of his office, she understood that they came from the same background, the same type of family.

This was not to discount certain things about him. Like the fact that no one had ever said anything close to the things he had said to her, in their warmth and depth of feeling. The problem was that he could express those feelings only when he thought she was asleep. The problem was that to access the warmest, most human part of him, she would always have to be partly unconscious.

In Ben's office, they were quiet for a long time. She could hear other employees shuffling out to lunch. She wanted to join them. The conversation was going nowhere. She would have to shock him.

She unzipped her skirt. "What are you doing?" he asked uneasily, glancing at the door. And then: "What is that?"

"An arm." She explained what the doctor had told her, how this was not uncommon.

"I've heard about this on the news." He was staring at it, transfixed. "I've just . . . never seen it."

"It's real," she confirmed. "Do you want to touch it?"

As if on cue, the baby arm began to contract. It was no longer pink, but a mangled red color. It had grown a bit of peach fuzz. Even she felt taken aback, looking at it again.

"Not right now." He was polite in his repulsion.

"What are you afraid of?" It wasn't until this moment that she realized this was what she wanted, to be an aberration to him.

"Look, I know what you're doing," he snapped. "I'm not going to let you quit your job. Please, zip yourself up." He paced back and forth, irritated. "Here's what we're going to do." He outlined a plan that would enable her to use up all her vacation days at once. "You currently have six months of unused days. So take six months off."

"I thought the policy prohibits taking more than two weeks of vacation at once."

"I'll find a way around it," he said wearily. "But I have a condition. At the end of this, you have to come back. I'm serious about this. You need to return."

Why he needed this, she did not ask. "Well, I have a condition too," she said quickly, before he could change her mind. "I want to leave tomorrow."

It was Eve's first trip back to her home country alone, unchaperoned by her parents. She wanted a homecoming, whatever that meant. Maybe it was to be overwhelmed by déjà vu, a staggering tsunami wave. A first cousin once removed, who now lived in what was formerly England and with whom she traded holiday emails, had helped her get in touch with her great-aunt and to arrange a stay at her home. The great-aunt was a widow who lived alone, off her late husband's pension.

Eve was surprised to find, upon arriving from the airport, that her aunt's apartment was in a new-construction building modeled after a prewar New York residence, and wouldn't have looked out of place on the Upper East Side. At least until she encountered the interior.

The marble-tiled lobby consisted of a mishmash of European architectural styles—crown moldings in the shape of ivy leaves, a Tudor-style chandelier, and a set of trompe l'oeil paintings of Venetian windows. A mechanical baby grand played "Tiny Dancer" next to a koi pond. She kept circling, trying to find the elevator bank. There was no elevator in the entire place, it turned out, and a maintenance worker pointed to the door leading to the stairs. The stairwell lights flickered precariously as, panting, she clambered up to the sixteenth floor, her hidden baby arm flapping beneath her dress.

The apartment's double doors opened to the dining room, its table set with a wild tangle of food. Arranged around a pyramid of tangerines, there was sugarcane stuffed with sausage, a steamed fish covered with a mound of julienned ginger and scallions, a soup flecked with lotus roots, a shrimp and lychee dish, wilted spinach. Those were what she could see, all garnished with little dishes of various nuts and foil-wrapped toffee candies. Her great-aunt, a small, tidy woman in her seventies, stood next to the large table. She patted Eve's cheek shyly in greeting, then embraced her.

They no longer shared a common language, but cobbled together a rudimentary conversation as well as they could, with gesturing and pointing. When in doubt, they used the translation app on Eve's phone, and a disembodied British voice provided the linguistic bridge: *That sauce goes with the fish*, or *Be careful. You have a stain on your shirt.*

When they grew tired of trying to communicate, they took little bites from the oversized spread, so bounteous and sprawling that her aunt must have been expecting ghosts. She bit off a piece of tangerine, stinging with almond-soaked sugar. It turned out to be made of marzipan, garnished with gold leaf and filled with chocolate and nuts. She remembered, suddenly, New Year parties with her grandmother, her aunt's wedding, her own going-away party when she'd moved to the States. When the déjà vu came, it was like drowning.

The air-conditioning, blasting on high, turned on and off periodically without warning. Same with the lights, which flickered as if in a haunted house. The electricity in the building, her aunt indicated, was finicky and haphazard in the evenings. Suddenly, all the minor discomforts of jet lag, of pregnancy, of varied and rich foods, of fluctuating temperatures, of unreliable lighting, snowballed into a disorienting avalanche of dizziness, of fatigue. She felt woozy.

Next thing Eve knew, she was lying on the sofa, the ceiling lights still blinking above, and her aunt was taking off her shoes. Eve murmured that she was sorry for forgetting to take them off before entering, what a faux pas. The aunt laughed, said something Eve didn't catch, as her nimble fingers undid the shoelaces with slow, purposeful care. This aunt was essentially a stranger; they did not share the conflicts that Eve shared with her parents and others in the family. She had not been wounded by her in the same way. The idea of a beginning.

She was drowsy after overeating. As her aunt stroked her forehead, she thought that, yes, finally she understood what a homecoming was supposed to be. It was to be comfortable in a way you couldn't be elsewhere. It was to be mothered into an oblivious ooze.

214

Even still. When she felt the baby arm move, she shrank away from her aunt's touch.

Over the next few days, her aunt took her around her birth city. These were the sights she recognized from childhood: the stone bridge over a pond of lily pads, the sculpture park with a stone tiger she'd once posed beside as an uncle (divorced out of the family by now) took her photo, and the outdoor street market where her grandma used to buy morning groceries.

Aside from these sites, so much of the city had been knocked down and replaced with new developments. This was at least partly due to the effects of the de-Americanizing program, a state initiative to "reclaim" the country's true heritage and reverse undue Western influence. All American-owned businesses had been banned and replaced, often by imitative domestic counterparts. There was not a familiar chain or franchise in sight, though she spotted a few empty storefronts with ghost signage: a KFC, a pair of dismantled golden arches in an alley.

Yet America as a subliminal presence remained every-where, if not more strongly than before. An ideology de- _true_ fined only by what it opposes is doomed to be defined by that exact thing. Even if there were no more KFCs, the CFCs looked pretty much the same. And so America could be felt in the layouts and fluorescent lights of the supermarkets; the familiar, loud graphic designs of billboards, advertisements, product packaging; the gleaming surfaces of malls; housing developments modeled after the suburbs of Orange County; a White House–like building that, upon closer inspection, turned out to be a prison.

Even though English had been banned, kids liked to illicitly mouth "Cool" and "Okay" before being smacked upside their heads by their mothers. As for Eve, she kept her mouth shut in public. This was what she had done on previous trips back with her parents, who pointed out that her accent was obvious when she spoke, more like baby-talked, in her native tongue.

One evening, they were walking through an outdoor market when her aunt suddenly became animated and gestured in a certain direction. She pulled her niece's arm, quickening her pace. Through the crowded street, they zigzagged past vendor stalls, eateries with plastic dining sets, and open storefronts pumping pop music. Her aunt didn't have any problem jaywalking, playing chicken with intercepting motorists. Everyone did it here, but Eve was surprised by her relative's brazenness, the quick, loud snap of her plastic sandals against concrete. Her grip was surprisingly strong.

They went across an overpass. Below, motorists whizzed down the freeway, coursing at breakneck speed around other vehicles.

Across the freeway was an older, less-developed part of the city. The busy commercial district gave way to residential

housing, cloistered by ungroomed foliage and trees unhur-
riedly moving their arms in the breeze. The sound of traffic
became distant, replaced by the din of ambient noise: buzz-
ing insects, a garbage can lid closing. The streetlights were
few and far between.

Her aunt slowed down and stopped in front of a nonde-
script building in a concrete courtyard, lit up under a fluorescent streetlamp. It was older and more squat than the new
construction she kept seeing. People lived here, behind the
faded floral curtains. Her aunt pointed to one of the windows in the building, said something.

"What?" Eve was still out of breath.

Her aunt repeated the word insistently. Then again.

Eve took her phone out and recorded the word and ran it
through her translation app. The automated British voice rose
from the ether, filling the space between them: *Birth*. The app
repeated the translation: *Birth*.

She looked at the building again, at the corner window
on the second floor. The place of birth, she understood. Her
birth.

Her aunt asked something to the effect of "Do you remember?" An absurd question, but she did not strain when
she answered, "Yes. I remember." Even though it was impossible, she did remember.

A shadow moved behind the curtains, someone passing
by to retrieve something in the front room, maybe a cup of
tea now grown cold, a pair of house slippers in need of a

wash. In the courtyard outside bloomed a thicket of magnolia trees. They reminded her of the magnolias in Lafayette Square, where she and Ben used to take lunchtime walks. He didn't like even his shadow to publicly touch hers. Beneath the leaves, he would study the ground instead.

The great aunt said something else. Too tired to cobble together her meaning, Eve ran it through the app again. The voice, in Eton-trained English, emanated from the ether again: *Isn't it better to be back?*

"Yes," she responded in her native language. "Yes, it is."

In the middle of the night, Ben wrote her an email. He had woken up from a dream about her. He was walking with Eve through Lafayette Square during lunch hour, something that they actually used to do. It was mostly the feeling of her presence that stayed with him, the scenery of the flowers all around them, and his anxiety about things left unsaid.

This was how the message had begun. It was uncharacteristic of him to refer to his dreams, much less feelings, which he once explained he viewed as natural phenomena, just tides lapping the shore.

Then the tone became a bit more clipped, more brisk, lapsing back to his tendencies. He asked her about health, and how things were. He updated her on happenings at the office, and then assured her that if she had any trouble, whatever it was, he would help.

The email, sent from his work address, turned out to be a functionary piece of correspondence. He reminded her that her six months of vacation days were almost up, and they really should iron out a plan for how to proceed when she returned. He included the date when she would be required back at work, as if she might've forgotten, then signed off with "Warmly."

He hit SEND before he could spend too long finessing his words.

Her nighttime ritual after her shower was to dress the baby arm. She stored its caretaking materials in a canvas sachet, wrapped with a string. After drying the arm with a muslin towel, she would warm up a dollop of protective pink ointment in her palm, before spreading it across its skin. Then she distributed a few drops of an oil blend and lightly patted it into the skin. The arm looked fat and big now, the flesh firmer than before. She gave it a little massage. Every week, she trimmed its nails.

In the streetlight shining through the bathroom window, she liked to look at the baby arm before she put on its warmer, a tiny weighted sleeve that restricted its movements and calmed its occasional nervous shaking, like a ThunderShirt. It seemed to respond to her attention and care, to exhibit enjoyment. What had at first seemed grotesque was now just lovable. Whatever misgivings she had had about being

219

a mother seemed moot when confronted with this pudge of appendage, no less chonk in its flesh rolls than those sported by most "normal" babies.

This was what she was doing when her aunt, bearing a stack of folded towels, walked into the bathroom.

There was silence. It seemed plausible that the revelation of the baby arm could be met with sympathy, or at least acceptance. But the towels dropped to the floor. The aunt's frozen smile held as she slowly backed out of the bathroom into the darkened hallway, the electricity having switched off.

Retreating into the hallway shadows, her aunt began shaking her head, her eyes darting around before settling again on her great-niece in disbelief, then disapproval. There it was. This expression was familiar to Eve, reminiscent of the way her parents, grandparents, aunts, and uncles had all, at one time or another, looked at her. It was a look of dismay and confusion, as if they didn't know what to do with her, couldn't quite claim her as their own.

The shadows fell over her aunt, enshrouding her until she was no longer visible. All Eve could hear was her voice— some cries, unintelligible things. No translation app was needed to understand.

Why did she feel so galvanized into pleading her own case? Still naked, not even having tucked a towel around herself, she took a few steps into the hallway. To the darkness, she explained that she had seen a doctor, that this prenatal "defect" was, if not normal, then at least not a cause for alarm. It was very common in America. Other pregnant women suffered this too.

There was no answer. She was not sure if her aunt was still there, or if she had slipped away to somewhere else in the apartment.

As Eve stepped into the hallway, an arm shot out of the dark, grabbing her by the neck. It was a small, ancient arm, wiry and wizened, but strong. It tightened around her, and would not give as she attempted to pry its fingers off. She struggled to take in air. The baby arm flailed around helplessly, a flopping fish, setting off a series of contractions.

A seething voice came out of the dark, associated with no one, no one that she could see. *Get out. Get out.*

She thought she was going to black out, but then realized it was her own panic, her raspy breathing, that had seized her throat. The hand had eased its grip around her neck. Its strength was firm but not life-threatening, not deadening. Her family would only wound her, nothing more, so that she went through this life maimed, but still she went through life.

Eve finally stepped out of its grip, convulsing with humiliation, rippling with contractions. Through it all, she could feel the baby arm shaking. Retreating into the safety of the bathroom, she soothed and petted the little arm, cooing to it as it shook with stress. Its fingers curled around hers. They had just been warm-up contractions, not real ones.

The humiliation she felt was followed by anger. This doesn't matter, she thought. None of this mattered because she would return to the US, where she would give birth to her baby, the first in the family to be born an American citizen. He would be free from his lineage of demanding ancestors, free from their restrictive traditions and expectations. She could withstand the brutality of this moment for the lucidity it brought her: she would never return. She would never come here again.

She glared out into the darkened hallway.

Get out. Get out.

Right, and what else was new? Tomorrow couldn't come fast enough.

When her reply arrived, weeks after his email, it too came in the middle of the night. It was a brief message. She apologized for not responding sooner, but she had been traveling. She said that her health was fine, and that she had been staying at a relative's, and was now staying in a hostel. That was it.

In reply, he asked her, Are you planning on returning? He reminded her once again of the date she was expected back in the office. He was deciding, he added, how to delegate a few upcoming projects, and was counting on her return.

There was no immediate response. And then, a few days later, a response that was barely a sentence: Yeah, of course.

Her assigned gate at the airport was still boarding another flight. There were three hours to kill before her return to DC, but she didn't want to pay for another night at the hostel just to stay a few extra hours. This is how she found herself in the boarding area close to midnight, on a weeknight, watching local news programs play across multiple screens.

The current flight boarding at her departing gate was to Chicago. The passengers had mostly been processed, their boarding passes scanned, with only a few stragglers rushing with luggage as the gate was closing.

On the TV, the newscaster kept referring to the *imperialists*, as translated in the closed captions. During her time here, she had learned that the term was virtually synonymous with *Americans*. The current segment, presented with somewhat triumphant flourish, was about how the birth rate in the US was down from previous years. But then, Eve thought, wasn't that the trend in almost every developed nation? She dozed off to the broadcaster's descriptions of imperial decline, trying to remember where she had read that.

She woke to the sound of a man's voice yelling, "Wait! Hold on!" It had been so long since she had heard any form of American English that she automatically roused. It was the siren call of the familiar. A middle-aged couple was rushing toward the gate, wheeling their squeaky carry-on suitcases.

"That's our flight!" the woman yelled at the attendant.

"Too late," the attendant told them, as they neared. "We closed. Five minutes ago."

Outside, the plane had disconnected from the Jetway. The couple looked back and forth between the attendant and the plane, the attendant and the plane.

"No, no. We need to get on," the man said decisively. Midwestern, Eve could tell from their accents. But maybe from the more liberal bastions of the Midwest, at least based on their bearing. The silver-haired, bespectacled husband wore a white button-up under a navy blazer, and the wife was in a light-gray dress of natural fibers and dyes, accessorized with a delicate, probably responsibly sourced gold necklace.

"We need to be home," the woman added.

"Gate closed," the attendant answered calmly. "We rebook."

The couple nodded, quiet for a moment as they looked, almost serenely, at the plane outside, lights blinking in wait. The silence, it turned out, was less acceptance than recalibration. They erupted.

"For God's sake, it's right there!" The husband gestured to the plane outside the window, its doors fully closed. "They can just open the door again. You can just let us through."

"We've been here for two weeks!" the wife stated. "We can't stay another day. I'm allergic to the heat. The water is full of bacteria. I can't eat the food here!"

In the boarding area, there were other passengers sitting around, likely waiting for the next flight too, young expats who had scored cheap flights at inconvenient hours. They watched this exchange with unease and morbid curiosity.

One of the travelers tried to intervene. Walking up to the couple, the stranger offered assistance. "Do you need help getting to the ticket counter? You can get another ticket at the counter upstairs, and I'm sure they'll book you on the next flight."

The wife didn't seem to hear. She might've been talking to herself when she announced, "I miss our house, and our friends and family. I just want to go back to our country! We have to see our dog! Our—our children!" She was crying now, her bracelets jangling as she moved her hands to her face.

"You people are known for your hospitality!" the husband added. "This isn't hospitable!"

Eve looked around. Was this a joke? She would not have been surprised to find a camera crew filming for a prank show. Or perhaps they allowed themselves to behave this way precisely because they did not think anyone was watching. Outside of the US, they were finally free.

That's when she felt a contraction, a real one this time, red and laser-focused, moving from the top of her uterus down to her pelvis, body horror in a sci-fi movie. She stiffened, afraid to move. It lasted less than a minute, but it was a focused pain this time, a kind that she hadn't felt before.

"You can't go on the plane. The door is closed." The attendant's obligatory smile was fading. "Door closes, no boarding."

The wife looked out the window pleadingly. "But the plane is right there!"

Eve felt the baby arm move, scraping at her skin, as if in warning. "Not now," she muttered to herself. "Please, not now. Any other time than this." She crossed her legs, gently pinning the arm between her thighs.

"C'mon," the husband persisted. "Just use your walkie-talkie and tell the pilot there are two passengers they missed." He paused. "The plane is right there!"

"Reschedule." The attendant was now quiet in his authority. He picked up the phone and called someone. "Security," he requested.

"We just want to go home. We just want to go home," the woman said, weeping. The sound of her sobs seemed to echo around the terminal, bouncing off the window that reflected the scene back to everyone watching. The baby arm had freed itself from her crossed legs, was flailing once more, digging at her skin. In the moment before Eve felt another contraction, the plane turned and headed out. She watched, dully, as it glided down the runway, speeding toward liftoff.

Acknowledgments

The term "bliss montage" was, to the best of my knowledge, coined by the film historian Jeanine Basinger. I was inspired by her writings on the topic in *A Woman's View*.

Thank you to Jin Auh and the team at Wylie, including Luke Ingram, George Morgan, and Elizabeth Pratt. And molto gratitude to Jenna Johnson and Stephen Weil at FSG, along with Janine Barlow, Lianna Culp, Daniel del Valle, Nina Frieman, Debra Helfand, Hillary Tisman, Claire Tobin, Caitlin Van Dusen, and the many others who have worked on this book.

Other versions of these stories have been published by *The Atlantic*, *Granta*, *The New Yorker*, *Unstuck*, *The Virginia Quarterly Review*, and *Zoetrope*. My thanks to the editors: Cressida Leyshon, Oliver Munday, Luke Neima, Michael Ray, Paul Reyes, and Matt Williamson.

I would not have been able to take time off from teaching

without generous support from the Whiting Foundation and the National Endowment for the Arts. This book exists with their help. Ucross Foundation provided reprieve at the right time.

I keep afloat with support from friends, a few of whom read early drafts of these stories. Thank you, Daniela Olszewska Beer, Will Boast, Nick Drnaso, Dan Genoves-Sylvan, Isabelle Gilbert, Jacob Knabb, Katie Moore, Harper Quinn, and Kirsten Saracini. Thanks to my mom for the long months of extreme caretaking. And to Valer for being, always, my best reader. And to Vlad, a person I could not have dreamed up or imagined.

A Note About the Author

Ling Ma is a writer hailing from Fujian, Utah, and Kansas. She is the author of the novel *Severance*, which received the Kirkus Prize, a Whiting Award, the VCU Cabell First Novel Award, and the New York Public Library Young Lions Fiction Award. She lives in Chicago with her family.